KING OF THE
SEVENTH GRADE

OTHER LOTHROP BOOKS BY BARBARA COHEN

BENNY
THE BINDING OF ISAAC
BITTER HERBS AND HONEY
THE CARP IN THE BATHTUB
GOOSEBERRIES TO ORANGES
I AM JOSEPH
THE INNKEEPER'S DAUGHTER
QUEEN FOR A DAY
R MY NAME IS ROSIE
THANK YOU, JACKIE ROBINSON
WHERE'S FLORRIE?
YUSSEL'S PRAYER

KING OF THE SEVENTH GRADE
by Barbara Cohen

LOTHROP, LEE & SHEPARD BOOKS
NEW YORK

Library of Congress Cataloging in Publication Data
Cohen, Barbara. King of the seventh grade.
Summary: Thirteen-year-old Vic hates Hebrew school and is indifferent
to his upcoming bar mitzvah, until he is suddenly disallowed from
participating in either. [1. Jews—Fiction. 2. Bar mitzvah—Fiction] I.Title.
PZ7.C6595Ki [Fic] 82–15247
ISBN 0–688–01302–3 AACR2

FOR LEAH COHEN
AND STEVEN CHATINOVER

CHAPTER ONE |

Pretty soon I was going to be sick to my stomach. I was actually going to vomit, sitting right there in the classroom. That was one way, anyhow, to get out of the place I had long ago decided was the armpit of the universe.

Because what was I doing there on a gorgeous October afternoon, listening to Mr. Hyman, the world's number one creep, drone on in his flat, nasal, boring voice? I should have been out in the fields behind the middle school playing football, or hanging out at the shopping center with the other guys.

I was there because I was almost thirteen. Being thirteen is funny. It's funny queer and funny ha-ha. If you're Jewish, it usually has an extra added attraction —a bar mitzvah. *Bar mitzvah* means "son of the commandment" in Hebrew. If you're a girl, you don't have a bar mitzvah; you have a bat mitzvah. That means "daughter of the commandment."

The ceremony is supposed to mean that you're grown up. Obviously, you're not really grown up at thirteen. You may wish you were, or even think that you are, but none of the real grown-ups are fooled for a minute. Still, they're the ones who're so sold on the whole bar mitzvah business.

Actually, the rabbi and the Hebrew School teachers explain to you that becoming a bar mitzvah (the ceremony and its leading player go by the same name) just means you're grown up so far as the Jewish religion is concerned. It means you've accepted all the responsibilities and rituals of an adult Jew. You show that you're ready for this by getting up in front of the entire congregation in the synagogue on a Saturday morning and chanting in Hebrew a portion from one of the prophetic books of the Bible. You have to read the one that's scheduled for that week, the same one they've been chanting on that particular Saturday for the last two thousand years. You do not get your pick. If you did, everyone would read Haftarah Vayyakhel, which is the shortest, and no one would read Haftarah Beshallach, which is the longest.

Like most kids, I got to be thirteen the year that I was in seventh grade. It turned out to be a very complicated year. Now that I look back at it, I laugh about it—sort of. I didn't laugh much at the time.

At the beginning, as I said, the whole bar mitzvah business made me want to throw up. I felt that if I had to listen to Mr. Hyman for one more minute, I'd either throw up or scream. But, of course, I did neither. I had other ways of getting a little fun out of those endless, miserable afternoons Pop insisted I spend in Hebrew School.

I poked Howie, who was sitting on my right. "Get ready," I whispered. "Tell the others."

Obediently, Howie nudged Morty and whispered to him. Morty nodded and passed the message along. In a moment all the boys, and several of the girls, had taken pencils out of their pockets or purses and were holding them in their hands.

Mr. Hyman was reading from a book called *The Life of a Jew*. Every student in the class had a copy of the book, but Mr. Hyman read it out loud anyway, instead of telling us to read it to ourselves. In the beginning, he had assigned chapters, first for homework, and then to be read in class, but it hadn't taken him long to realize that even if he walked up and down the rows, staring first at one kid and then at the next, most of us simply refused to read what he had told us to read. So now he read out loud.

He looked up from the page. "All right," he said. "Let's see who's been listening. According to Jewish law, what makes a person Jewish? How do we define a Jew?"

No one raised a hand.

Wearily, Mr. Hyman sighed. Then his eyes roved around the room. I felt safe. Mr. Hyman wouldn't call on me. Ever since the day I had led all the other kids out of the room and into the hall for five minutes in the middle of class, I think Mr. Hyman had been afraid of me. That's not saying much. Mr. Hyman was afraid of a lot of things—drafts, germs, rock music, and more than two seventh graders at once. He never looked at me if he could help it.

"All right, Morty," Mr. Hyman said. "Would you please answer my question?"

"What was your question, Mr. Hyman?" Morty asked. His voice was pleasant and reasonable.

"What makes a person Jewish?" Mr. Hyman repeated. "How do we define a Jew?"

"My goodness, Mr. Hyman," Morty said, as mildly as before, "how would I know a thing like that?"

"Morty, I've just spent the last ten minutes reading the answer to that question out loud." Mr. Hyman actually had tears in his voice. He often seemed to have tears in his voice. I almost felt sorry for him. "If you'd done as I'd asked, and opened your book to the page I was reading from," he went on, "you'd have the answer in front of you this very minute."

"Well, I don't know the answer," Morty retorted. "And to tell you the truth, I don't care."

"You don't care?" Mr. Hyman's voice shot up to a peak of shrillness. "You don't care? If you don't care, what are you doing here?" He must have known as soon as the words were out of his mouth that he'd said the wrong thing. Mr. Hyman was a whiner and a creep, but he wasn't dumb.

"I'm here because my parents make me come," Morty replied. "Believe me, Mr. Hyman, if it was up to me, they could take this whole bar mitzvah business and shove it."

"If you can't watch your language, Morty," Mr. Hyman said, "I'll have to send you to see Rabbi Auerbach."

"What's wrong with the word *shove?*" Morty muttered. "It's not a bad word." But he was giving up. No one wanted to be sent to see Rabbi Auerbach. I didn't like Rabbi Auerbach much better than I liked Mr. Hyman, but I could not describe Rabbi Auerbach as either a whiner or a creep. He could make even me nervous. He'd been at the temple for only a year. The congregation had fired the one before, Rabbi Gross. No one had been afraid of Rabbi Gross. He was more of a Mr. Hyman type.

Mr. Hyman was still nudzhing Morty. "Just answer my question," he said.

"I told you," Morty replied shortly, "I don't know the answer."

A hand shot up suddenly. It was Abby's. Abby the priss. One or two of the other girls would have answered Mr. Hyman's question if they were called on, but only Abby would volunteer. I disliked her more than I disliked Rabbi Auerbach and nearly as much as I disliked Mr. Hyman. But I didn't hate her. She was only a girl, and not worth that much energy.

Mr. Hyman smiled. "Yes, Abby?" he asked.

"My father says a true Jew is a human being who tries to be a mensch," she said.

A *mensch*. A man. It was one of the two or three Yiddish words, like *nudzh*, that I actually knew. I knew them because they were in my father's vocabulary. "Stop nudzhing me. Be a mensch, for once," he would complain when I did something that annoyed him, which was just about every other minute. Be a man. But it couldn't just mean "be a man." If that's all it meant, that's what Pop would have said. "Be a man, for once." But instead he said, "Be a mensch."

"I agree with your father," Mr. Hyman replied, still smiling. "We'd all be better Jews if we understood the true meaning of *menschlikeit.* But the passage I read to you today deals with the definition of Jew according to Jewish law, the technical definition, as it were."

"I don't like that definition," Abby said firmly.

Abby was Mr. Hyman's pet. He didn't get mad at her because she disagreed with something in the book. He merely said, "Well, you don't have to like it, Abby. All I'm asking is that you tell me what it is."

"Oh, all right, then," Abby said. "According to Jewish law, all you have to do to be Jewish is be born of a Jewish mother."

"Unless you convert," Seema chimed in. Hard as it was to believe, those girls actually seemed to be interested in the subject.

"Yes," Mr. Hyman said. "If you're not born of a Jewish mother, you can become a Jew by undergoing the process of conversion. But those are the only two ways." Mr. Hyman turned around to write what he'd just said on the board, leaving his thin back, clad in a faded blue turtleneck shirt, exposed to the class.

"Now!" I said. I kept my voice low, but it could be heard all over the room. My pencil was in my hand. I began tapping it rhythmically against the top of my desk.

At the same instant, almost everyone else in the class

14 |

did the same thing. *TAP tap tap, TAP tap tap, TAP tap tap, TAP. TAP tap tap, TAP tap tap, TAP tap tap, TAP.* Over and over again, over and over again, like rain beating against a windowpane.

Mr. Hyman whirled around, his pale face flushed red as fire. "Stop that!" he screeched, his voice high and uncontrolled, as it always was when he was angry. "Stop that this instant!"

But no one stopped. *TAP tap tap, TAP tap tap, TAP tap tap, TAP.* "Stop, stop," he screamed. All the while that he screamed, we went right on tapping. Then he stopped screaming and tried to talk in a more normal tone of voice. He was breathing hard, though, and it was difficult for him to get the words out. "You'll stay in this room until the tapping stops," he sputtered. "I don't care if the bell rings, you'll stay here. I'll begin teaching the lesson again when this outrage ceases." He sat down at his desk. The tapping continued without pause. *TAP tap tap, TAP tap tap, TAP tap tap, TAP.*

"You can't make us stay here, Mr. Hyman," I called out, above the sound of the tapping. "We go home in car pools. Our parents won't let you keep us after six o'clock."

"Rabbi Auerbach will back me up," Mr. Hyman said. "Your parents will back me up, too. They won't let you get away with this. So you'd better stop tapping right now. I don't care if I have to sit here until midnight. I'm getting through today's lesson today, no matter what." *TAP tap tap, TAP tap tap, TAP tap tap, TAP.*

No one moved. No one said anything. But our hands were busy. *TAP tap tap, TAP tap tap, TAP tap tap, TAP.*

And then the bell rang.

Every kid in the classroom stood up. Every kid in the classroom marched out the door. Even Seema. Even Abby.

I took my time. I wasn't in any hurry. No one was waiting for me. I didn't belong to a car pool. Pop hadn't arranged one for me. I rode my bike home. I strolled toward the door, behind all the others. I didn't care if I was the last one out of the room.

Suddenly I felt a hand on my shoulder. I didn't like being touched. I whirled around and saw that it was Mr. Hyman who'd grabbed me. Before I could warn him to keep his hands off me, he'd let go. All he had wanted was my attention. "Vic, would you please stay behind for a moment," he said. "I'd like to speak with you." His voice was quiet.

"I don't mind," I said. I sat down on one of the desks in the front row, stretching my legs out in front of me. "What do you want to know?"

Mr. Hyman was standing directly before me. I looked into his eyes; he shifted his gaze. "It was you who started that pencil-tapping incident—" he began.

"How do you know?"

"Don't interrupt me." He was trying, without much success, to sound tough.

I shrugged.

"I know it was you." He answered my question, anyway. "I heard you say 'Now' just before the tapping began."

"You can't be sure of that, Mr. Hyman. It could have been anybody." My tone was kind.

"But it was you," Mr. Hyman insisted. He didn't sound kind at all. "You're the one who thinks these things up. You're the ringleader. The rest just go along with you."

I scratched my ear. "So what do you want me to do? You want to send me to Rabbi Auerbach? I'll go. You can't prove anything, anyway." I didn't want Mr. Hyman to think for one second that I was afraid of Rabbi Auerbach. And I wasn't afraid of him. I just didn't need any hassle.

"No, I don't want you to go to Rabbi Auerbach," Mr. Hyman said. "What's the point?"

"Yeah," I agreed. "What's the point?"

He lowered his skinny rump onto the desk next to the one on which I was sitting. When he spoke, his voice wasn't angry anymore. It was full of a hearty friendliness as phony as a three-dollar bill. "Vic," he said, "what're you doing in Hebrew School? Why don't you just quit?"

"My father makes me come," I told him. "It's the same with all the kids. Their folks make them come. They don't like it."

"That may be," Mr. Hyman agreed, "but if it weren't for you, they'd put up with it. I wish I had half the power over them that you do."

For a moment I didn't know what to say. Was Mr. Hyman trying a new tactic—flattery? But then I thought of the right words. "You know, Mr. Hyman, if it wasn't me, it would be someone else—Morty, maybe, or maybe even Howie."

"But a lot of the kids like the idea of a bar or bat mitzvah," Mr. Hyman said. "A party, hundreds of presents. So they put up with Hebrew School as the necessary preliminary."

He was living in dreamland. "Some of the girls, maybe," I said. "The boys, no. If they could have the party and the presents without Hebrew School, that'd be OK. But all the presents in the world aren't worth killing two afternoons a week in this dump, plus an extra half hour or so to practice your haftarah with the cantor. All the guys feel that way."

"You took maybe a survey?" Mr. Hyman asked sarcastically. Whenever he thought he was being funny, he put on a plastic Yiddish accent—plastic because Mr. Hyman, for all that his hair was receding and his shoulders were hunched, was only in his mid-twenties and had been born and bred in Elizabeth, New Jersey.

"If they felt different, would they go along with me?" I asked reasonably. I knew that was a tacit admission of my ringleader role, but it didn't matter. Mr. Hyman couldn't do anything about that, either.

"It's against the rules around here to admit to wanting a bar mitzvah or anything else to do with Judaism," Mr. Hyman said. "That doesn't mean that, deep down, lots of kids aren't really looking forward to the big day. Not every thirteen-year-old gets to be a king for twenty-four hours. You have to be Jewish. Mrs. Rifkind tells me that last year Howie and Ira and some of the other boys were excellent students."

"Mrs. Rifkind is an excellent teacher," I retorted. That was a lousy thing to say, but it was true. The bright red color that was an infallible guide to Mr. Hyman's emotional state suffused his face once again. He'd gotten the point.

"Seventh graders are difficult," was all he said.

"I thought it was me," I reminded him. "I thought you said it was all my fault."

"It's the combination. I think it would be better if you left. It would be better for the class, and it would be better for you."

For once he and I were in perfect agreement. "Why don't you talk to my father?" I suggested. "If you can convince him, I'll be grateful to you till the day I die."

"Maybe I will call him," Mr. Hyman said. "But I'll have to talk it over with Rabbi Auerbach first."

Well, that was the end of that. I knew Rabbi Auerbach would never consent. He believed that as long as a kid came to Hebrew School, as long as he had a bar mitzvah, there was a chance, however slim, to save him for Judaism. If he didn't come, there was no chance at all. Rabbi Auerbach couldn't possibly agree to actually inviting a student to withdraw.

"In the meantime," Mr. Hyman said, "I want a promise from you. I want a promise that you'll behave."

I looked Mr. Hyman right in the eye. As before, his glance fell away. I didn't say anything. He didn't say anything else, either. He just let out his breath in a long, windy sigh.

I stood up. "Well, good night, Mr. Hyman."

He grunted something, I wasn't sure what. I walked out the door, making sure to slam it hard behind me. The corridor was empty. I ambled past the classrooms, past the rabbi's empty office, past the cloakroom. The door to the combination library and chapel was open. I could hear sing-song male voices chanting in Hebrew. The sound was ragged and disorganized, not like a choir, but still, somehow, musical. It was the minyan, the quorum that gathered morning and evening for prayers.

I had time. My father wouldn't be home for half an hour and, when he did get home, he wouldn't be surprised or upset at not finding me there. We each took care of our own dinner, eating together only one Sunday a month when he took me to a Chinese restaurant, or on an occasional Friday night, when we went to my grandmother's.

I slipped into the chapel. There were no more than a dozen men gathered in the room, and that included Rabbi Auerbach, Cantor Itkin, and Mr. Perle, another Hebrew School teacher.

I sat down at an empty table in the rear. No one seemed to notice me. I picked up one of the prayer books lying on the table. It was different from the prayer books used on Saturday mornings. I flipped through the pages, but I couldn't find the place.

The rabbi wasn't leading the service. He was sitting at one of the tables, just like the other men. The service seemed to be going along more or less by itself. On holidays, or at bar mitzvahs on Saturday mornings, the rabbi stood in front and announced the pages. Everyone knew what was going on.

But here, at the evening minyan, I was lost. I was angry, too. I had been coming to Hebrew School twice a week since we'd moved to New Hebron a little over three years before. That came to more than four hundred hours of Hebrew School. Four hundred and twenty hours, to be exact. In four hundred and twenty hours they hadn't taught me enough Hebrew so that I could figure out where a congregation was when it was praying. Not that I really wanted to know. It was just proof that the whole thing was a waste of time, even from the point of view of people who cared about it.

The men continued to utter their low, oddly musical words. They stood up for a while and prayed silently, their lips moving, their bodies gently swaying to private rhythms. The silent prayer was called the Amidah. I knew that much. I felt a little better. I turned the pages rapidly. English translations ran alongside the Hebrew, and I was able to locate the page headed "The Amidah is said standing in silent devotion." But I didn't read the words. In spite of three years of Hebrew School, it would have taken me fifteen minutes to get through one page of Hebrew. I didn't see any point in bothering with the English, either. God hadn't done so well by me lately. What was the point of praying to Him?

When the first couple of men sat down, I sat down, too. In a few moments, they were all seated. Then they said some prayers together. The rabbi led them, but not from the front of the room. He just stayed were he was, at the table. But his voice was the loudest, and he started first.

I began to feel bored. What was I doing there? Why had I wandered into the room? Curiosity, I guessed. When I left Hebrew School at the usual time, the minyan hadn't yet begun, so I'd never noticed it before. This time, alone in the corridor, I had noticed it. So I'd come in. So now I knew. So it was time to go.

I wasn't acquainted with most of the men in the room, but I did know the rabbi, the cantor, and Mr. Perle. I didn't want them to notice I'd been there. I didn't want them to comment on my presence or speak to me. I didn't want to start anything with them.

I waited to leave until everyone was occupied. When the tiny congregation began singing the closing hymn, "Adon Olam," "Lord of the World," I got up as quietly as I could. I shut the prayer book and moved it toward the middle of the table, where some others were piled. Then I straightened up. As I did so, I saw that Rabbi Auerbach had turned his head. He was looking right at me. He was looking right into my eyes. He wasn't smiling, he wasn't frowning. His face was calm, his dark eyes piercing. Hastily, I ducked my head and slipped quickly out of the room.

I was annoyed with myself. What had possessed me to go into the minyan? All I had learned was that Hebrew School was a waste of time, which I'd known all along. And I'd attracted the rabbi's attention. That could only have been a mistake.

It was cool out. A sharp wind blew around the corner of the synagogue building. I zipped up my jacket. My bike was in the rack, the only bike remaining. There never were many, anyway. Most of the kids came by car. The building was located in a suburban neighborhood without any sidewalks. Even those kids who lived near enough to walk or ride their bikes usually weren't allowed to do so. Their parents didn't like them coming home in the dark after Hebrew School along the edge of the road. It was too dangerous. I was one of the few permitted to go back and forth under my own steam.

I took my key ring from my pocket, knelt down, undid the lock, pulled the bike out of the rack, and mounted up. I pedaled down the long blacktopped driveway as fast as I could and swung out into the road with scarcely a glance to see what was coming. I bowled along with all the power my legs could generate. I wanted to feel the wind biting into my face. I wanted it to blow away all the cobwebs in my brain. I didn't want to think about anything, or feel anything, except the movement, and the wind, and the cold.

When I got home, the house was still dark. After I let myself in, I ran from room to room, turning on all the lights. Pop would be furious when he came home, but I didn't like being alone in a dark house. I didn't care if he got mad at the waste of electricity. He made plenty of money. He could afford to pay the bill.

I went into the kitchen, opened the refrigerator, and stared at the shelves for a long time. They contained a carton of milk, a moldy salami, half a dozen cracked eggs, two six-packs of beer, a package of American cheese, half a loaf of white bread, a wrinkled tomato, and three dried-up apples.

I took the carton of milk out of the refrigerator. From the cabinet underneath the stove I pulled out a box of Sugar Pops. I poured some into a bowl that I retrieved from the dishwasher, added some milk, and carried the bowl and a spoon into the family room, where I snapped on the TV. I shoveled the cold cereal into my mouth, scarcely tasting it. My eyes were glued to a rerun of *Happy Days*, and I kept my mind glued to it, too.

The cereal was gone, but I still hadn't moved from

my seat in front of the TV when I heard the door open between the garage and the kitchen. Pop was home.

I stayed where I was. I heard him slam the door, walk into the kitchen, drop his briefcase onto the table, and then walk through into the family room. "For crissakes, Vic," he said as soon as he saw me, "how many times do I have to tell you I don't own stock in Amalgamated Gas and Electric Company? I'm not made out of money. Why the hell are all the lights on?"

I continued to stare at the TV. Fonzie was romancing a girl motorcyclist.

"Vic, I asked you a question. Why the hell are all the lights on?"

Still I said nothing.

He reached over and snapped off the TV.

"Hey, Pop," I protested, "I was in the middle."

"When I'm talking, Victor Abrams, you'll kindly listen. Go through the house and turn off every light."

"Then can I finish watching the show?"

"Yeah," Pop allowed, "I guess so. Though how you can stare all night at this crap is beyond me."

And what he watched wasn't crap? Reruns of old Phil Silvers and Lucy shows on UHF channels aren't crap? But I did as I'd been told. Now that he was home, I didn't need all the lights anyway. But I couldn't possibly tell Pop that. I couldn't tell anybody that.

When I was done with the lights, I wandered back into the kitchen. Pop was taking a beer and the American cheese out of the refrigerator. "I had a bite at the station, before I left the city," he said. "Did you eat anything?"

"Yeah, some cereal. Listen, Pop, can't you get some decent food in this house?"

"You got a bike," Pop replied shortly. "Go downtown and get what you want. I'll give you the money."

But he and I both knew that I would do no such thing. I didn't know where to get started in a supermarket. For that matter, neither did he. We did our meager shopping at 7-Eleven or Wawa or some other convenience store.

"Mom's been gone a year and a half," I said. "You'd think by now we'd be managing a little better around here."

"We're managing OK," Pop replied defensively. "I can't see that anything's the matter. Mrs. Harter keeps the house clean. I got two promotions, now that I can concentrate on my job. You don't like the food in the house, you've got the money for restaurants. We're as good as we've ever been. I guess your mother is, too. There's nothing to complain about."

He was right—right about my mother, that is. She was happier. She hadn't liked being married to my father. He wasn't very exciting. They'd never done anything, never gone anywhere during their marriage. Even I liked her new husband, Bart Levine. He always had interesting, funny stories to tell me, when he sat still long enough to carry on a conversation.

So my mother was happy. And my father said he was happy. But I wasn't so happy. "Listen, Pop," I said. "I've got to quit Hebrew School. I can't stand it anymore. I don't want to be bar mitzvahed anyway."

"We've been over all of this before," Pop replied

wearily. "I told you, you can't quit. Your cousins were all bar mitzvahed, and you're going to be bar mitzvahed, too. You're not going to be my mother's only grandson not to have a bar mitzvah." He sat down at the kitchen table and pulled the top off the beer bottle. "Especially now that I can afford a really classy party."

I sat down across from him. I would try a new tack. "I think Hebrew School's beginning to interfere with my regular schoolwork," I said. "Wait till you see my report card this quarter. It'll be way down." It wouldn't be hard to make that happen, if I had to.

"You're smart enough to handle Hebrew School and regular school both," Pop replied in a flat, even voice. "Don't try any funny stuff. If I find out that you're cutting Hebrew School, or if I see a bad report card, no more allowance." He gave me twenty dollars a week. No other kid I knew got that kind of allowance. I spent every penny of it, on myself and on my friends, and a lot of it at McDonald's, where I ate supper three or four nights a week. "I'm tired of trouble," he added sharply. "I'm tired of one teacher or another calling me up every other day to complain about your behavior." He was exaggerating. There'd been only two calls since school had begun, and they were both back in September, while I was still shaking down some of the teachers. But I didn't know if he'd actually carry out his threat to cut off my allowance. I didn't intend to put him to the test. I'd find another way.

I stood up. "Where're you going?" he asked.

"Upstairs, to do my homework."

"I thought you were going to watch the rest of *Happy Days.*"

I'd forgotten all about *Happy Days,* which was over by then, anyway. I was amazed at Pop's memory for irrelevant detail. "Don't forget," he went on, "Grandma wants us to come for dinner Friday night."

"Mom and Bart are home," I said. "They're expecting me this weekend."

"Oh. Grandma will be disappointed." But Pop raised no further objection. The agreement between my parents gave them joint custody of me. I hated the term *joint custody.* It sounded as if I were a jailbird.

Originally, it had been intended that I would spend every other weekend with Mom. In practice, it had worked out quite differently because Mom and Bart were away so much. When a weekend did come along that I could spend with Mom, Pop couldn't very well object. We never had any plans together, anyway. Pop spent much of the weekend at the apartment of his girlfriend, Mrs. Kirsch. He would have been perfectly satisfied if I had been away many more weekends than I was, because then he could have brought Mrs. Kirsch to our house much more often. He never had her sleep over when I was home.

I walked out of the kitchen. "You're sure they're expecting you?" Pop called after me.

"Yeah, I'm sure," I replied, without stopping or turning my head.

But I wasn't sure at all. As soon as I was out of Pop's sight, I raced down the hall and up the stairs into my own room. I had my own extension. I dialed my mother's number.

Bart answered the phone. "Hi, old man," he said. "How're you doing?"

"Great, Bart. How're you? Did you have a good trip?"

"Super, old man, just super. What can I do for you?"

"You're expecting me this weekend, right?"

"Oh?" Bart seemed to hesitate. "I'll put your mother on. You can straighten it all out with her."

A moment later I heard Mom's sweet, soft voice. That voice fooled a lot of people. It masked a will of iron. "How are you, darling? It's so good to talk to you again. Miss me?"

"Sure, I missed you," I said. "Did you miss me?"

"Terribly," Mom replied. "I thought of you every day."

"All I got was one postcard."

"I can't understand that." She sounded aggrieved. "The mails are a disgrace these days. I wrote from every city. The letters must have gotten lost."

"I was surprised you didn't call."

"Oh, darling, there just wasn't time. But now I'll be home for a while, and we'll spend whole long days together."

"How about this weekend?" I asked quickly.

"Oh, darling, this weekend we're so booked. You know how it is when you first get home."

I didn't.

"But, of course, you're welcome," she added hastily. "You're *always* welcome. It's just that we won't be here much."

"That's OK, Mom," I said. "I'll come anyway. I need a change of scene."

"As dull around there as ever, huh?"

"Well, you know. . . ."

"Yes, I know." I heard the dryness in my mother's voice that always showed up when Pop was under discussion. "Come on over, honey," she said. "I'll stock up on lots of goodies. We won't be home for dinner, but I'll leave a tuna-fish casserole and a pot roast in the fridge for you. All you'll have to do is heat them up. Invite friends over, if you like."

I wondered if I could put my hands on the key to her house. It had been a long time since I'd used it. As soon as I hung up the phone, I looked in the little cedar box that sat on top of my chest of drawers. It held a handful of shells from the vacation at the beach the three of us had once taken together, an 1898 silver dollar, two high-powered shooters that I couldn't part with even after I gave up playing marbles, and a whole bunch of tie tacks and cuff links I'd gotten as birthday presents and never worn. I found the key, too, attached to an old Boy Scout key ring. I'd never even belonged to the Boy Scouts. I was a Cub Scout dropout. The key ring was another long-ago birthday present.

I sat down at my desk and did my homework. It didn't take long. Then I watched *Soap.* I didn't have to leave my room for that because, in addition to my own phone, I had my own TV.

About ten-thirty I heard Pop clump up the steps on his way to his bedroom. I didn't bother to call out "Good night." Neither did he.

CHAPTER TWO |

"Hey, Vic," Pat said, "come with us after school. We're going over to Playland. They got in that new game, Galaxia. Stewie told me."

I shook my head. "I can't," I said gloomily. "I got to go to Hebrew School."

"My God, Vic," Pat groaned, "how much longer are you going to put up with that stuff? Regular school is bad enough. They used to make me go to catechism class until I was confirmed. That was only half an hour a week, and even so I couldn't stand it. A bar mitzvah is sort of like being confirmed, isn't it? Why does it take so much time?"

"Jews have to do everything the hard way," I said. I began unwrapping one of the ice cream sandwiches I had on my tray. Two others lay there, waiting. That was all I planned to eat. School lunch that day was Spanish rice. To me it looked like maggots, and I wasn't having anything to do with it. I wouldn't go near the cheese or the watery tuna-salad sandwiches, either. They looked worse than the stuff in our refrigerator.

"Do you have to have a bar mitzvah?" Pat asked. "I mean, will they throw you out of being Jewish if you don't?"

"I don't think they can throw you out of being Jewish," Big John chimed in. "I think it's like being tall or fat or having freckles. You're born with it."

"Something like that," I agreed. "But don't worry. I'll find a way of acing this Hebrew School business, if it's my last living act."

"We're not worried," Big John said with a laugh. "We have total confidence in you."

"What're you going to do?" Pat asked.

"I haven't decided yet," I told them, "but it'll be something good."

"Why can't you just tell your old man you don't want to go?" Big John suggested. "Why don't you just tell him you don't want a bar mitzvah?"

"I tried that, jerko," I snapped. "He ain't buyin'. I may not want the bar mitzvah, but he does. He's got to show those snobby brothers of his, and their snobby wives, and their snobby, snobby kids, and I'm the one who has to suffer for it."

"Show them what?" Pat asked.

"That he's perfectly OK even though my mom left him," I shot back. "That he's got just as much money as they have. All that kind of stuff."

"A bar mitzvah will show them that?" Pat sounded thoroughly mystified.

"The party, stupidhead," Big John informed him kindly. "The party will show that."

"You kikes are crazy," Pat said.

"You micks are dumb," I retorted.

"Come outside and say that," Pat countered, putting up his dukes.

I half rose from my seat. "OK. Let's go."

"Oh, lay off, Pat," Big John said. "You know Vic could beat you with one hand tied behind his back."

"I'd like to see him try," Pat muttered, but at the same time he took a big bite out of the fat ham-and-Swiss-cheese sandwich on a seeded hard roll that his mother had packed for him. The discussion went no further. It never did. To Pat and me, *kike* and *mick* scattered through our conversation didn't really mean anything more than *jerko* and *stupidhead*.

"Hey, guys!" That was Stewie, pulling out the chair at the head of the table and plopping himself down on it, hard.

"Hey, Stewie, where you been?" Big John asked. "Lunch is almost over."

"Old Criddlepuke kept me back. She had to talk to me, she said." Old Criddlepuke was Miss Criddlepaugh, who taught pre-algebra to seventh graders.

"What about?" I asked.

"My attitude. She doesn't like my attitude. Well, if she doesn't like it, she knows what she can do with it."

I laughed. Miss Criddlepaugh didn't like my attitude, either, but she gave me A's anyway. She was fair.

"It's that mealy-mouthed Abby Greenglass," Stewie said. "Old Criddlepuke asked her if I'd copied her homework, and she said yes."

"Did you?" Big John asked.

Stewie stared at Big John in amazement. "Of course. Everyone copies Abby Greenglass's homework."

"I don't," said Big John.

"That's because you're not in pre-algebra, dummy."

"Well, what did you want Abby to do, lie?" Big John asked.

"You would have lied, wouldn't you?" Stewie asked.

Big John didn't reply.

"People like her don't know the rules," Stewie complained. "They don't know anything about loyalty."

I felt uncomfortable. I tried to figure out why. Abby Greenglass was one of my least favorite people. I wasn't going to open my mouth to defend her. But I wondered what kind of loyalty Abby Greenglass was supposed to owe Stewie Brisbane. What had he ever done, or what would he ever do, for her?

I stood up. "Leaving so soon, darling?" Stewie asked, putting on the falsetto voice that always made all the guys laugh.

"I gotta go," I said.

"Well, when you gotta go, you gotta go," Stewie chirped.

I managed a smile.

"They got the new Galaxia game at Playland," Stewie said, returning his voice to normal.

"Yeah," I said. "Pat told us."

"We'll see you there, after school."

I shook my head. "Not me."

"Poor old Vickie has Hebrew School," Pat said.

"Cripes," Stewie said. "I thought you'd outgrown that stuff by now."

"I'm going to get out of it," I said. "Soon."

Stewie laughed. "I hope it's soon. Because when you're not there, I can't afford to play."

I reached in my pocket and took out a dollar bill. I laid it on the table in front of Stewie. "Here," I said. "A loan."

Stewie looked up at me, a curiously unpleasant expression on his face. Then he looked down at the money, as if it might bite him. But after a brief moment, he reached out his hand and closed his fingers around the bill. He put it in his pocket without bothering to say "Thanks," or "I'll owe you," or "You'll get it back as soon as my old man pays me for cleaning the yard." Stewie rarely paid me back, but he usually talked as if he intended to. Today he hadn't bothered. I thought I knew why. It was probably because I'd embarrassed him by giving him the money in front of the other guys. Maybe I shouldn't have done that. But it had seemed to me that Stewie was asking for it.

I walked across the lunchroom, carrying my tray in one hand, while I wadded up the ice cream sandwich wrappers in the other. About ten feet from the garbage pails I wound up and threw the wad toward the nearest container. It arced gracefully through the air and landed right where it belonged. Some sixth grade boys sitting at a nearby table applauded enthusiastically. "Watch yourself, boy," said Mr. Stanhope, the cafeteria monitor, who was leaning against the wall, arms folded across his chest. If I'd missed, Mr. Stanhope would have ordered me to pick up the wad, which I might have done and might not have done, depending on how I felt. I wouldn't have minded being assigned detention. Detention was no worse than Hebrew School.

Maybe it was better. At four-thirty that afternoon, I found myself wishing that I had missed the garbage pail, that Mr. Stanhope had asked me to pick up the wad of paper, that I had refused, that Mr. Stanhope had assigned me detention, and that I was at this very moment walking around the school yard carrying a big plastic bag, which I'd be filling with papers, the usual punishment for litterers. It was raining, but I thought even the rain would have been preferable to Mr. Hyman's droning, monotonous voice. He was chanting the prayer that preceded the haftarah. We were supposed to be chanting it along with him, since we'd all have to do it the day of our bar and bat mitzvahs. But the only voices other than that of Mr. Hyman himself were a few of the girls', most prominently Abby Greenglass's, who really was just as creepy as Stewie claimed.

The time had come to make my move. I had decided what to do. Pop would be mad. He might again threaten to cancel my allowance. But I figured I could get around that by telling Pop that Bart said he'd give it to me instead. Pop would never allow such a thing, so he'd go on paying me. And this new idea would operate much faster than my earlier plan of screwing up my report card. As a matter of fact, it should work instantaneously.

As soon as Mr. Hyman reached the end of the prayer, I stood up. "Hey, Mr. Hyman," I called out. I kept my tone casual, but very loud. As soon as I spoke, the murmuring whispers, which were a constant undertone in the class, suddenly ceased. All eyes were on me, including Mr. Hyman's.

"You know, Mr. Hyman," I said, "as a singer, you suck."

The familiar flush spread out from Mr. Hyman's cheeks all over his face, turning his pale, freckled skin bright red. The class emitted a single gasp, as if everyone in the room had drawn in a breath at once. Some of the kids were pressing their lips together, trying to swallow smiles. Others looked shocked. Even Howie and Morty looked a little shocked, although I'd told them before class to expect something. "I'm going to get out of here for good today," I'd said. They'd wanted to know how, but I wouldn't tell them. As a matter of fact, I hadn't known myself what my exact words were going to be until I'd said them.

Mr. Hyman walked down the aisle. He grabbed me by the upper arm. I shook myself free. "Don't you touch me," I spit out in a low tone.

"Get out of here," Mr. Hyman said. He pointed toward the door. "Get out of here this instant."

I obeyed. After all, it was what I wanted. But I didn't rush. I sauntered toward the door very slowly, as if I were strolling around the shopping center on a sunny Saturday afternoon with the gang. When I got to the door, I pushed it open. Then I turned around and looked at Mr. Hyman. "Excuse me, Mr. Hyman," I said very politely, "but where should I go? Home?"

"Go to Rabbi Auerbach's office," Mr. Hyman said. "I'll see you there after class."

Unaccustomed silence still reigned in the classroom. I stepped out into the hall. I knew everyone was waiting for me to slam the door, so I closed it very carefully, turning the knob until I could feel the latch soundlessly slide into place.

I walked down the hall at the same easy pace. I sauntered into the rabbi's outer office. "Hi, Mrs. Kadin," I said cheerfully.

"Hello, Vic," Mrs. Kadin greeted me. She was the rabbi's secretary. She knew every kid in the school. "What'd you do this time?"

I lowered myself into one of the large black chairs on the opposite side of the room from Mrs. Kadin's desk. "Mr. Hyman said I was to wait here for him," I replied. I didn't say any more. She didn't have to know everything.

"Are you supposed to talk to the rabbi?"

"He didn't say that."

Mrs. Kadin's forehead creased in a frown, but she kept quiet. She turned back to her typewriter and to the stencil she was working on.

I picked up a magazine from the coffee table and tried to read it. It was a very boring magazine. All the articles had titles like "The New Role of Women in Synagogue Life" or "A New Interpretation of the Laws of Tumah." I thought I might just leave. That's what I'd intended to do at first. But then I'd decided against that. It would be better to get it all over with, to be officially and finally tossed out, beyond my father's ability to do anything about it. And I was sure that was what would happen. There was no way, no way in the world, they could let me get away with what I'd just said. Not in a Hebrew school. Not right after a prayer.

I could hear voices through the closed door to Rabbi

Auerbach's study. The rabbi was in there, talking to someone, maybe to two people. I strained my ears in an effort to hear what they were saying. But I couldn't make out a word, only the rise and fall of voices growing louder and softer, softer and louder.

After a while the people came out. It was a young couple. They were smiling and holding hands. Perhaps they had been talking about their wedding. They said good night to Mrs. Kadin and left. The rabbi stayed in his study.

Several times, the phone rang. Mrs. Kadin answered. She switched some calls into the rabbi. Others she took care of herself. Occasionally a kid walked into the office, sent by a teacher looking for some supplies or information. When not taking care of callers, Mrs. Kadin clacked away at her typewriter. She did not consider it part of her job to help me pass the time.

The hour until the end of the Hebrew School session passed very, very slowly. I realized I'd made one mistake. I should have saved my rebellion for later in the period.

But at last a little alarm clock on Mrs. Kadin's desk produced its insistent ring. She shut it off and then turned and pushed a button on the wall behind her desk. A loud buzz sounded throughout the building. Almost instantly the place was alive with noise. Doors opened, voices and footsteps sounded in the hall, parents walked in and out of the office on errands they'd combined with picking up their kids. Mrs. Rifkind, Mr. Perle, and the other two Hebrew School teachers stopped in to pick up their mail. Mrs. Rifkind ran off a ditto on the machine for the next day's class. Miss Blaustein asked Mrs. Kadin to order some more copies of her class workbook. Mr. Zaretsky took a pack of construction paper out of the supply closet.

But then that burst of liveliness died down, too. Mr. Perle went inside to talk to the rabbi. Mrs. Kadin put on her coat and left. Old Mr. Surowitz poked his head in the door. "Where's the rabbi?" he asked.

"In there," I said, gesturing toward the study door. "With Mr. Perle."

"Tell them we're starting the minyan," Mr. Surowitz said. "Tell them we got ten men without them, they can take their time." I opened my mouth to object. I wasn't going to just walk into the rabbi's office uninvited. But Mr. Surowitz was gone.

A moment later Mr. Hyman finally walked through the door. He looked at me for a second before he spoke. "You're still here," he said. He sounded almost surprised.

"You told me to wait for you," I replied.

"Well, we'll go in to see the rabbi now," Mr. Hyman said. It was obvious that the prospect did not delight him.

"Mr. Perle is in there," I offered.

Mr. Hyman sat down heavily. He rested his elbow on the arm of his chair, covered his face with his hand and shut his eyes. It was obvious that he didn't want to talk.

But when Mr. Perle and the rabbi walked out of the inner office together, Mr. Hyman was on his feet in an instant.

"Mr. Surowitz came by," I reported. "He said to tell

you they have a minyan, and you don't have to rush."

"Go ahead, Myron," the rabbi said to Mr. Perle. "I'll be along in a few minutes."

Mr. Perle nodded and left the room. The rabbi sat down on the sofa. "What's the problem, Mr. Hyman?" He sounded as tired as Mr. Hyman looked. He gestured as he spoke, indicating that Mr. Hyman should take his seat again. "The usual, I suppose. Wouldn't it be nice," he added almost dreamily, "wouldn't it be nice if you were here to discuss some aspect of halacah, of Jewish law? Wouldn't it be nice if you and Vic were about to ask me if it was all right for Vic to play football on the Sabbath, or to discuss the meaning of some passage in his haftarah? Wouldn't that be nice?"

I almost laughed out loud. The poor rabbi was going crazy. I played football or not on Saturday, just as I pleased, without consulting the rabbi or anyone else. And I didn't care beans what my haftarah meant. I hadn't even looked at it since the cantor had given it to me a month before.

"We're here to discuss a very serious matter, Rabbi," Mr. Hyman began.

"Vic's haftarah isn't a serious matter?" the rabbi asked, smiling faintly.

"That's not what I mean, Rabbi." Mr. Hyman bristled defensively.

The rabbi was teasing Mr. Hyman. Maybe he was just as tired of Mr. Hyman, with all his whining and complaining, as I was. One of the rabbi's jobs was serving as principal of the Hebrew School. Principals are never fond of teachers who can't control their classes themselves and must constantly send their students down to the main office. Principals like teachers who are good disciplinarians. And the funny part of it is, so do kids, as long as the discipline is neither demeaning nor unfair.

"Then why are you here, Mr. Hyman?" the rabbi asked mildly.

"This boy has behaved in a totally unforgivable way," Mr. Hyman said. "I will not have him back in my classroom. I will resign before I permit that."

"What did he do?" the rabbi asked.

"He used unforgivable language to me," Mr. Hyman said, flushing again at the memory. "Totally unforgivable language. Vile. In front of everyone, the girls too."

I restrained a snort. When I was in third grade I had had that particular meaning of that word explained to me by Debbie Barton, a girl who now sat in the front row between Abby Greenglass and Seema Katz, her fair, angelic beauty giving no hint of her currently even more extensive and colorful vocabulary. She was a cheerleader, and Stewie Brisbane was crazy about her.

The rabbi turned to me. He looked quite interested. "What did you say?" he asked.

"I said," I repeated slowly, "I said, 'Mr. Hyman, as a singer, you—' "

"Stop!" Mr. Hyman exploded, his voice rising to its shrill screech. "If you use that word again in my presence, I'll . . . I'll . . ."

"Calm yourself, Mr. Hyman," the rabbi said. "Calm yourself. Vic won't say the word. I get the idea."

"The boy should be thrown out of Hebrew School,"

Mr. Hyman insisted. "He should not be bar mitzvahed. He's not a Jew. He's a barbarian."

"He can be a barbarian and still be a Jew," the rabbi replied quietly. "Unfortunately, the latter does not preclude the former."

Mr. Hyman was calmer now. He shook his head firmly. "Rabbi," he said, "this boy knows nothing of Jewishness, nothing of Jewish values."

"But that's *our* job, isn't it?" the rabbi said. "A human being can be born a Jew, but he's not born a mensch. That he has to learn. And we're supposed to teach him —you and me."

A terrible thought crept into my head as I listened to the rabbi's unaccountable words. It was possible that he was not going to throw me out of Hebrew School. I had thought I'd done something that even he, who hung onto each student like a leech, would find unforgivable. Not the word itself, but the terrible disrespect to a teacher that the public use of it implied. Principals might not like teachers who couldn't discipline their own classes, but unless the teacher had done something illegal, like beat a kid up, or make a pass, principals almost always stood behind teachers. If they didn't, they were afraid the discipline of the whole school wouldn't survive ten minutes.

"Do you know the word I used, Rabbi?" I interjected hastily. "I said—"

"I know what you said," the rabbi interrupted. "I served in the United States Army during the Korean War. I am over eighteen and am therefore allowed into R-rated movies. I am, in other words, a citizen of the

United States during the last quarter of the twentieth century. I know what you said."

"And you're not going to throw me out?" As soon as I said those words, I would have given the next month's allowance to have them back. I had made a fatal mistake. I had let the rabbi know I wanted to be thrown out. After so many years of experience dealing with teachers and principals, how could I, who was usually so smart, have done such a dumb thing? Never let the enemy know what you really want, because if they know they'll be sure to give you just the opposite. Obviously, there was something disconcerting about Rabbi Auerbach. He had thrown me so thoroughly off my guard, I had forgotten Rule Number One.

"Throw you out of what?" the rabbi asked.

"Out of Mr. Hyman's class," I replied carefully.

"Mr. Hyman has already thrown you out of his class. You're not to go back."

Mr. Hyman heaved a sigh of relief. So did I. I had guessed right, after all. A principal had to back up a teacher, even a teacher he didn't respect.

"Instead," the rabbi continued slowly, "you will report to me on your Hebrew School days. I'll teach you myself."

"But Rabbi Auerbach—"

"What's the problem?" He smiled a little. "Don't you think I can handle it?"

"Rabbi Auerbach, I don't think you understand." I was desperate. "Mr. Hyman is right." This was unbelievable. Mr. Hyman had suddenly become my ally. "I don't belong in Hebrew School. I don't deserve to be bar mitzvahed." That was the right tactic. Turn the whole thing into a moral issue.

Rabbi Auerbach brought the tips of his fingers together thoughtfully. "If we all got only what we deserved, there wouldn't be much hope for any of us," he said. "Fortunately, God does not deal with us merely as we deserve. He's merciful as well as just."

If Rabbi Auerbach was in the business of imitating God, I was in a lot of trouble. "I hate Hebrew School," I said, very slowly, very clearly. "I don't want to be bar mitzvahed."

Rabbi Auerbach's forefingers tapped each other gently. "That doesn't have much to do with the matter, either."

"My father makes me come," I said. "He *forces* me."

"Look at it this way, Vic," the rabbi said. "If anyone had asked you when you were, say, eighteen months old whether you wanted to use the toilet, you'd have said no, you preferred your diapers. But your father—and your mother—made you use the toilet. You're not sorry about that now, are you?"

"Rabbi, I haven't the slightest idea what you're talking about," I snapped. What kind of religious type was Rabbi Auerbach, anyway, talking about God one minute and toilets and diapers the next? I'd bet that Pat's priest, Father Spencer, didn't talk about things like that. Of course, I didn't really know Father Spencer, so I couldn't be sure what Father Spencer would talk about. It appeared I didn't really know Rabbi Auerbach, either.

"I hope you know what you're doing, Rabbi," Mr. Hyman said.

"I hope so, too, Mr. Hyman," Rabbi Auerbach replied, an edge to his politeness. "Perhaps I'm making a mistake—"

"You are, you are," I interrupted.

The rabbi ignored me. "But if I am, it won't be the first one, or the last one. And if it doesn't work, no harm done."

"No harm done?" Mr. Hyman sounded as if he couldn't believe his ears.

"Sticks and stones may break my bones," Rabbi Auerbach chanted softly, "but names will never hurt me."

"I wouldn't rule out the possibility of violence," Mr. Hyman said through thin lips.

"Well, I would," Rabbi Auerbach replied firmly. He turned to me. "Let's see—today's Wednesday. That means you have Hebrew School again on Monday. Our first session will be on Monday, then. Come at your regular time."

I looked the rabbi straight in the eye and shook my head very slowly. I said quietly, "Don't wait for me, Rabbi Auerbach. I'm not coming."

Rabbi Auerbach's eyes did not turn away. "You'll be here," he returned, his voice calm and pleasant. "I'm calling your father. I'm asking him to come to see me Monday, too. Also your mother."

"You can't have my mother and my father at the same time!" I exclaimed in horror. "They're divorced." They couldn't even speak over the telephone without getting into a fight.

"Divorced from each other," the rabbi said. "Not from you. The four of us will talk together about you and Hebrew School and your bar mitzvah. I think that's the best idea."

"All right," I said, suddenly struck by a new thought. "Have it your way."

Mr. Hyman threw me a suspicious glance. "He has something up his sleeve, Rabbi. Mark my words."

The rabbi chose to ignore that remark. He stood up. "Minyan must be almost over. Shall we drop in anyway, Mr. Hyman?"

Mr. Hyman stood up too. "Well, good night, Vic," Rabbi Auerbach said. Mr. Hyman didn't say anything. The rabbi walked out of the room. Mr. Hyman followed close behind.

I remained in the black chair for a long moment, thinking. It was going to be all right. On Monday, Mom and Pop would be in the same room. They would have a knock-down, drag-out fight, rabbi or no rabbi. I would make sure that fight would have one certain result—my release from bar mitzvahs and Hebrew schools and the whole damn synagogue building from that day forth as long as I lived.

CHAPTER THREE |

I peered into Mom's refrigerator. Even though she'd been home only a few days, it had a lot more stuff in it than my father's. I pulled out a loaf of raisin bread, a package of cream cheese, and a quart of milk. I dropped two pieces of the raisin bread into the toaster and sat down at the kitchen table to wait for them to pop.

It was after ten, but Mom and Bart weren't up yet. They had left for New York soon after I'd arrived the previous afternoon. I'd known they'd be leaving, but I had come anyway, in order to avoid another Friday night supper at my grandmother's house, listening to her rave on about what wonderful boys all her *other* grandsons were, how they wrote to her, and how they called her up, and how they sent her little gifts on her birthday. That was because they didn't live in the same town with her, and never had to endure Friday-night suppers of tasteless potted chicken, burnt kugel, and congealed rice. Other people's grandmothers were good cooks, at least. Mine didn't have even that single redeeming feature.

I'd fallen asleep before Mom and Bart had gotten home. Now I dawdled over breakfast, reading the sports section of the newspaper, hoping Mom would get down before it was time for me to go off to the shopping center to meet the guys. I wanted the chance to talk to her.

I bit into the raisin bread and chewed it slowly. I loved the mixture of flavor and texture created on my tongue by the rich, bland cream cheese, the crisp toast, and the soft, sweet raisins. When I was little I had come out from the city to spend weekends, sometimes, with my grandparents. Grandpa had always given me raisin toast and cream cheese for breakfast. I hadn't minded going over there when he was alive. In the summer we went fishing together, or for long walks downtown that always climaxed in chocolate ice cream cones. In the winter we spent hours in his workshop out back, where the smells of sawdust and shellac mingled together in my nostrils. Whenever I had supper at my grandmother's, I always went out back to see that everything was OK. I still had the key on my ring. I'd checked it out just two weeks before. The tools were still arrayed on the rack above the table, with perfect neatness, as they'd been when Grandpa was alive. But now they were covered with dust. I'd touched the adz. Its edge was dull. I'd sniffed hard, imagining that I could still smell sawdust and shellac.

Even when I was very little, Grandpa had always

made me do things. "Sand this chair rail until it's smooth. Hammer this nail straight into this board. Remove this screw with the Phillips head screwdriver. Cover this stepstool with a fresh coat of red paint."

Sometimes I complained. "I'm tired of sanding. I can't finish."

"What are you?" Grandpa would ask. "A man or a mouse?"

I always answered, "A mouse."

And Grandpa would always laugh. "No, you're not. Go up to the house and get some Oreos out of the cookie jar—two for you and two for me. Then come back and finish sanding."

An hour later the sanding or the painting, or whatever it had been, would be done. "What are you now, a man or a mouse?" Grandpa would ask.

I'd shake my head.

"You're a man," Grandpa would say. "A mensch."

Grandpa had died when I was nine, a year and a half before the divorce. It was good he hadn't lived to see that. He'd liked Mom a lot. Sometimes I think he liked her even more than he liked Pop, though Pop was his own son. I couldn't help remembering Grandpa when I was eating chocolate ice cream or Oreo cookies or raisin toast spread with cream cheese. Had Grandpa introduced Mom to that delicious combination? No, it must have been the other way around, because raisin bread and cream cheese were no longer available either in Pop's or Grandma's house. But I never failed to find them in my mother's refrigerator.

I was dropping two more pieces into the toaster

when I heard my mother's footsteps on the stairs. She came into the kitchen wearing a man's blue silk bathrobe. The pocket bore the initials BL embroidered in gold thread. Her curly hair was tousled, her eyes were full of sleep, but she still looked beautiful. She always looked beautiful.

"Morning, darling," she said. "I'm glad you found yourself some breakfast." She sat down at the kitchen table. "Be a love and put up some coffee. I can hardly move myself."

I measured coffee out of the canister on the counter into the electric pot that stood beside it. Pop always drank instant coffee in the morning, but Mom hated instant coffee. "You were out late last night," I said.

Mom nodded. "We went to a disco after the theater. Of course, we all drank too much. And then the noise. I thought my eardrums were going to collapse."

"Why did you go, then, if you didn't want to?" I returned to my seat, leaving the coffee pot to go about its business by itself.

"Well, I didn't want to be the old stick-in-the-mud who spoiled the party. Bart wanted to go, and so did the Edelmans." She smiled. "They didn't have a little boy at home they wanted to eat breakfast with in the morning."

"You don't have to eat breakfast with me," I said. "I'm almost done, anyway. You can go back to bed." I almost choked as I said those words.

"Oh, I'm up now," Mom responded cheerfully. "I'll be fine once I have some coffee. And I've got so much to do before Bart and I leave for the hockey game. The Vitales are picking us up at four."

"Don't you and Bart ever take a day off?" I asked.

She patted my hand. "I'm making up for all the boring years, darling. Can you understand that?"

"Yeah, I guess so."

"But this summer we're going to spend two weeks in the mountains, just eating and sleeping. The Colters are lending us their cabin. You can come with us for one of the weeks, if you want to."

"That'd be swell, Mom. Bart wouldn't mind?"

"Bart's crazy about you. You know that." She glanced toward the coffee pot. "The red light's on," she said.

I brought the pot and a mug over to the table. She poured the coffee and then took a deep sip. "It really makes me happy that Bart likes you, and you like Bart," she said. "It's so much easier for me this way."

"Oh, I like Bart a lot," I assured her. "When I grow up, I'd like to travel all over on business, and take my wife along, the way you and he do."

Mom nodded, a satisfied look on her face. "Yes, putting up office buildings is a lot more interesting than being an accountant. He's involved in so many different things, too. He doesn't spend all his spare time watching old sitcoms on TV."

When she talked like that, I got a little nervous. It seemed disloyal to listen to Mom knock Pop. No matter how hard they might fight when they met or spoke on the telephone, Pop rarely said anything against Mom to me, even though he might appear to have more cause, since it was she who'd walked out on him, and not the other way around. "What Pop does is OK, too," I said. "He's gotten two promotions in the last year and he's making plenty of money now."

"So I heard," Mom replied. "I'm really glad for him. I'm glad for you, too."

"There's only one thing wrong with it," I said slowly. "Now he can afford a big, fancy bar mitzvah party, and that's what he wants. He absolutely insists that I be bar mitzvahed. And Mom, I hate it," I exploded. "I hate every minute of it."

"I know that, too," Mom replied. "Rabbi Auerbach called me."

"Already?" I was surprised. I'd hoped to get to her first.

"Well, the meeting with him and you and your father is Monday. He spoke to me yesterday morning."

"Are you going?"

"Of course," she replied, a frown wrinkling her forehead. "I'm your mother, aren't I? When we moved back to New Hebron and enrolled you in Hebrew School, your father and I agreed you should have a bar mitzvah. You didn't hate Hebrew School then."

"Everything was different then." Maybe I sounded a little bitter.

"You still mad about the divorce, Vic?" Mom's voice was gentle. "Just because your father and I don't love each other, doesn't mean we don't both love you."

"Oh, Mom," I sighed, "I'll always be a little mad over the divorce. I know you had to leave him, I know what he's like, but you can't expect me to be happy about it."

Her sigh matched mine. "No, I suppose that's asking too much. But I can't understand why you're against the bar mitzvah, all of a sudden."

"It's not all of a sudden. I've been against it for a long time now. It's all a waste of time."

"You never told me."

I stared at her, hard. "I never had the chance. This is the first time we've actually sat down and talked in six months."

Her face looked as if I'd stuck her with a needle. "That's not true, Vic. You're exaggerating."

I could have proved that I wasn't, but since I wanted something from her, it wasn't the right moment for an argument. "Look, Mom," I said, "I don't want to be bar mitzvahed. I can't do my homework as well as I should because I have to go to Hebrew School. The teacher there's so bad I don't learn anything. I don't want a big, fancy party, because it won't have anything to do with me. It'll be for Pop and all his crummy relatives—"

"Like your Uncle Milton and your Aunt Helen," Mom interrupted. She didn't like them much, either.

I nodded. "The snobs."

"We had to move to this town when they were transferred," she said. "So your grandmother wouldn't be alone. That was the last straw."

"So you'll back me, Mom?" I pressed my advantage. "When we go to the rabbi Monday, you'll back me?"

"I'll think about it," she said. "I really have to talk to your father about it first. We always intended for you to have a bar mitzvah. We agreed on that."

"But it's me who has to have the bar mitzvah," I argued. "I think what I want ought to matter."

"Have you told him how you feel?" she asked.

"Of course I have," I retorted. "He doesn't care about my feelings."

"You can't imagine that he'll listen to me," she pointed out.

"Back me," I begged. "It'll be two against one, and then maybe the rabbi will see how ridiculous the whole idea is and go along with us."

"I won't promise you anything, Vic. I have to talk to your father first."

"Gee, Mom," I cried angrily, "all I'm asking from you is this one little thing, and even that's too much for you. I mean, really, you're just like him. You really don't care about the way I feel at all."

"Vic! How can you say that?" She looked as if she were going to cry.

"I can say it easy," I shot back, "because it's true." I got up from the table and stalked out into the back hall, where I took my jacket down from the coat rack and put it on.

"Vic, where are you going?" My mother was standing in the hallway.

"What do you care?" I opened the outside door.

She put her hand on my arm. "Vic, I insist. Tell me where you're going."

"To the shopping center," I said, my voice low. "I'm meeting the guys."

She seemed satisfied. She dropped her hand. "OK. Remember, you can bring some of them back here for supper. I left you a pot roast."

For an answer, I merely opened the door, stepped outside, and slammed it behind me. I went around to the shed next to the garage and rolled out my bike. I mounted it, and then I rode as hard and as fast as I could to the shopping center. It was five miles away, out along the highway, and I was late already.

CHAPTER FOUR |

Pat, Morty, Big John, and Stewie were waiting for me in front of the bakery, each one of them chewing on a fat doughnut. I locked my bike into the rack. Morty held out a paper bag. "Here, Vic," he said, "I bought one for you."

"Your buddy takes care of you," Stewie commented.

"Thanks, Morty," I said, reaching in for the doughnut. "How much do I owe you?"

"Forget it," Morty said with a wave of his hand.

"The rich guys always stick together," Stewie said. "You didn't tell *me* to forget it."

"Geezus, Stewie," Pat said. "What's eating you this morning?"

Stewie shrugged. "I'm broke."

"For a change," Big John said.

"Let's go over to Playland," I said. That's why we'd

come—to work the new video games at Playland. I'd lend Stewie money again, but this time I wouldn't offer it publicly. I didn't feel like annoying Stewie this morning. I wanted some peace and quiet.

We fooled around in Playland for about an hour. Then we bought some pizza and soda. We leaned against the front window of the pizzeria, chewing and sipping, and afterwards smoking cigarettes. "Let's go down to the school," Big John suggested after he'd drained the last drop from a can of birch beer. Big John didn't smoke. He was always in training for some sport or other. "We'll shoot some baskets. I can stop at my house on the way and get a basketball."

"Later," Stewie said. "Let's look in Radio Shack and Sound Effects and some of the other stores first."

"That's boring," Morty said. "I'd rather play ball."

"It's a lot more exciting than shooting baskets," Stewie contradicted.

"Oh, I don't know . . ." Pat said hesitantly.

"What are you guys, chicken?" Stewie asked.

"Me?" My back was up. "You're asking me if I'm chicken?"

"I'm not chicken," Pat protested. "I just don't want anything."

"But I do," Stewie said. "You guys got to come along for cover."

"If we ever get caught, my father will slit my throat with his own hands," Pat grumbled.

"We won't get caught," Stewie said. "Who gets caught? You know anyone who ever got caught? Everybody does it."

"Not *everybody*," Big John said.

"Everybody except a few creeps," Stewie amended. "You want to be a creep? Look, I'm not telling you to take anything. But I am telling you I need stuff, and you're going to go in the stores with me. You're my buddies, aren't you? We're a gang, aren't we?"

"Yeah, yeah," I said. I didn't like it when the guys in the gang had serious arguments. "Don't worry about it. We're coming. *Then* we'll shoot baskets."

The disagreement was over. We all walked away from the pizzeria together. Stewie led the way, pulling open one of the heavy glass doors that led into Woolworth's. The rest of us filed in behind him. We all knew what to do. We'd been shoplifting in an organized way for more than a year. Pat's father might have thought it was wrong, if he'd known about it, but what difference could that make to us?

I certainly had enough money to buy what I needed, and we'd lifted stuff so often it wasn't even very exciting anymore. But I knew we had to go into the stores before biking over to the playground to shoot baskets. I had to back Stewie. We all had to stick together. That was the point of the gang.

Once inside the five-and-ten, we spread out. If we hung around in a big bunch, the manager or a salesperson might get suspicious and make a point of keeping an eye on us. I stuck close to Stewie. Stewie wanted a birthday present for Debbie Barton. He wasn't going to get her anything too big—they weren't actually going out yet—just something to show he was interested. He decided on a pair of stuffed mice about three inches high. They were gray and soft. The female was dressed in a cap and apron, and the male wore a pair of overalls and a red neckerchief.

"They're cute, aren't they?" Stewie said.

"Yeah," I agreed.

"I think Debbie will like them."

"Why not?" I shrugged.

We moved over to the adjacent counter and pretended to be examining matchbox cars. I cased the area. It was empty of salespeople. Only two or three customers were close by, and they were engrossed in making their own choices. Of course, there were always the mirrors to worry about, but the mirrors caught shoplifters only when someone was looking into them, which, at the moment, no one appeared to be doing. "It's OK," I whispered.

"You take them," Stewie murmured in return. "You're closer."

With my eyes still on the cars, I inched my body toward the adjacent counter. My hand shot out and grabbed the mice. In an instant they were hidden away in the pocket of my jacket. I kept my hand in the pocket, too, holding onto the mice. As my fingers moved over them, I realized that, thinking I was picking up two mice, I'd actually picked up two pairs. The lady mouse and the man mouse in each pair were somehow joined together.

"Let's go," I said. It was our policy never to take more than a few items from one store at a time. The other guys were a couple of aisles away. When they saw Stewie and me turn to leave, they too made for the front of the store. Pat and Big John bought packages of bubble gum. You had to buy something. If you just walked past the cashier someone might wonder what you'd come in for in the first place.

Once out of the store, I gave Stewie one pair of mice. I didn't mention the other pair. Two pairs would have made a nice birthday present for Debbie, indicating, as one pair would not, that Stewie was really serious, but, unlike a piece of jewelry or perfume, preserving his reputation for coolness. I certainly had no use for two stuffed mice. But I held on to them, anyway.

We went into Sound Effects. It was a new store and the jerky managers hadn't learned yet that they had to keep tapes in locked cases. Stewie, Pat, and Morty all managed to palm a couple. In a place as busy as Sound Effects, they were too easy to steal to even consider paying for them, especially on a busy Saturday with too few salespeople around to service all the customers wanting help. Big John and I talked to the only clerk near the tape department. We pretended to be interested in buying a tape deck. It was a cinch.

In Radio Shack it was not so easy. The calculator Stewie wanted was locked away. The only stuff lying out in the open on racks were wires, ear plugs, catches, and other cheap little gadgets. Stewie contented himself with picking up three or four long-life batteries. "I can always use them," he told us when we were back out on the sidewalk.

"Hey, Stewie," Morty said, "let me have one. I need one for my pocket calculator."

"Nothing doing," Stewie said. "You want one, go in

and steal your own. I can use all of them in my tape recorder."

"Hey, Stewie," I said quietly, "we're all in this together, remember? Maybe it was you who actually palmed the batteries, but all the rest of us helped."

Stewie gave me a dirty look, but then he reached into his pocket and pulled out one of the batteries. Frowning and silent, he handed it to Morty.

Morty dropped it into his pocket. He didn't say anything, either.

Stewie led the way to Ekhart's Department Store. It was only a couple of doors beyond Radio Shack.

"What do you want to go in here for?" Big John asked. "There's nothing in here that we ever want."

Stewie shrugged. "It's close, we'll go in."

"By the time we get to the school, it'll be too dark to shoot baskets," Morty complained.

"This is the last store," Stewie bargained. "What d'ya say, Vic?"

I nodded. "OK. Then we'll get something to eat, and then we'll go over to the school."

We walked into the department store. The jewelry counter was directly opposite the main entrance. For some reason I couldn't understand, Stewie headed directly toward it. What could he possibly want with earrings and necklaces? He leaned his elbows on the counter and watched while a saleswoman helped a girl pick out a necklace. The jewelry counter was busy. Ekhart's was offering thirty percent off on all gold necklaces. Several were strewn about on the counter, and there were so many customers trying to attract the salesgirls' attention that I couldn't get close to the counter myself. I stood behind Stewie and waited.

Suddenly, he turned. He was smiling a little. His eyes moved toward the door. I understood. I followed him out of the store. In a moment, the others caught up with us. "You sure got out of there in a hurry," Big John said.

Stewie shook his head. That meant he didn't want to say anything right there in front of Ekhart's. We walked quickly to McDonald's. Lunch hour was over; the place wasn't crowded. We took a booth in the rear. Stewie sat with his back to the doorway. From out of his pocket he pulled two gold chains. He laid them on the table in front of him and surrounded them with his arms.

I guess my surprise showed on my face. So did Pat's and Morty's and Big John's. The price tag on one necklace read $189.98, marked down to $132.99. The other, shorter chain, had originally cost $155.98 and was now supposed to sell at $109.19.

"Geezus," Pat murmured. "Aren't you scared? I mean, they could put you in jail for that."

Stewie popped the necklaces back into his pocket. "It was easy," he whispered. "I just swept them off the counter. No one saw me, not even you, huh, Vic?"

I nodded. I was too shocked to say anything.

"What're you going to do with them? Give them to your mother?" Morty asked.

"Don't be stupid," Stewie said. "My old lady would be suspicious right away if I gave her an expensive present like this. She knows I'm always broke. I'm going to sell them."

"To who?" I asked. I was a little worried. I thought

Stewie could get in trouble for ripping off stuff as valuable as those necklaces. On the other hand, I had to admire him. He was cool, all right. "Anyone you sell them to might be just as suspicious as your mother," I pointed out.

"Don't worry," Stewie said. "I'll sell them. If any of you guys get anything big, just give it to me. I'll get rid of it for you, and we'll split the cash." He pulled a sharp, curved clipper from his pocket. "A guy I know gave me this. You use it to take off security tags so the alarm doesn't go off when you walk out of the store with the stuff."

Morty stood up. "It's kind of late," he said. "I promised my mom I'd clean the basement sometime. I think I'll have to skip shooting baskets."

"Don't you want something to eat?" Pat asked.

"I'm not hungry," Morty said.

"Not even for chicken?" Stewie asked pointedly.

Unsmilingly, Morty shook his head. He turned and walked quickly out of the restaurant.

"He's got no guts," Stewie said. "The big stuff scares him."

"If you want to know the truth, it scares me too," Big John said.

"Well, then, why don't you run home to mama, just like he did?" Stewie asked.

"Oh, shut up, Stewie," I said.

"Who are you, telling me to shut up?" Stewie shot back furiously. "You think you're the boss around here or something? Well, you're not *my* boss."

"I'm not anybody's boss," I said. I lowered my voice

to a whisper. "I just don't think it's smart to talk about this stuff in a restaurant." I stood up. "Everybody want a hamburger, Coke, french fries? I'll get them."

"I'll help you." Pat walked to the counter with me, leaving Big John and Stewie alone at the table. Big John was tearing a napkin up into little pieces. Stewie was staring off into space, his hand in the jacket pocket that carried the necklaces. I could see they weren't talking to each other.

Conversation didn't pick up much when Pat and I came back to the table. We ate our food quickly. "It *is* late," Pat said. "I think I'll skip basketball, too. We're all going to the movies tonight. I'd better get home."

"Yeah," Big John agreed. "Me, too."

I remembered the pot roast. "You want to come over and eat with me at my mom's house?" I asked Big John.

Big John shook his head. "My old man is taking my old lady out for dinner. It's their anniversary. I have to baby-sit my little brother. But you come on over to my house later, if you want."

"OK," I said. "Maybe I will."

Stewie's eyes moved from one face to the other. "I'm coming, too," he said.

Big John nodded. "OK, Stewie." The hesitation in his voice was barely noticeable.

"We're a gang," Stewie reminded him. "We stick together."

Later, when the others had gone, I sat alone at the table and thought about that. I was beginning to suspect that maybe Stewie had a different idea about the gang from mine. Sometimes Stewie seemed to think that the gang had to stick to him, but not that he had to stick to the gang.

I'd bought more french fries and more Coke. Unlike the others, I had no particular reason to rush home. It was after four. Mom and Bart had already left for the hockey game. I knew it would be better to wait to go over to Big John's until later. His parents weren't exactly crazy about me. They didn't seem to be exactly crazy about any of the guys in the gang.

I saw Abby Greenglass come through the door. She was alone, her arms full of packages. She recognized me and gave me a nod and a small, hesitant smile. I nodded back, but I didn't smile. Abby Greenglass was not entitled to a smile. She might take a smile as an invitation to sit down with me.

But just then a little boy raced through the door. "Buddy, stop it," his mother, chasing after him, called out. Buddy paid no attention. He tore down the aisle between the rows of booths and caromed off Abby, who stumbled, reached for the nearest table to balance herself, and scattered her packages all over the floor.

"Now look what you've done, Buddy," his mother scolded.

"I'm sorry," the little boy apologized. He didn't sound sorry at all.

"It's all right," Abby said. "No harm done." She bent down to pick up her bundles.

"Buddy, help the girl," his mother ordered. She couldn't help Abby herself. She was holding an infant in her arms.

"Oh, that's all right," Abby interjected hastily. "Let

Buddy go for his hamburger. He must be very hungry." Abby obviously felt that Buddy would be more of a hindrance than a help.

"But that's not right—" Buddy's mother began.

"I'll help her." I got up, bent down, and began gathering the scattered packages. Relieved, Buddy and his mother moved off toward the service counter. In a moment, all the bags and boxes were piled on the table where I had been sitting.

"Thanks, Vic," Abby said, standing up again. "I should have combined some of this stuff. I should have put the smaller packages into the bags with the bigger things." She began doing exactly that.

I slid back into my seat. "What'd you do?" I asked. "Buy out the shopping center?"

"I had to get a lot of things. My Young Judaea club is having an Israeli cafe at the Jewish Community Center tomorrow with the club from Rivington. I was in charge of buying everything—the decorations, the food, the favors—everything. I'll never let them stick me with all of that again," she added testily. "We should have divided it up." Now that she had everything neatly stowed in three large bags, she moved to pick them up.

"You can leave them here while you go get your food. I'll watch them." I sort of felt I had to say that.

"Oh, thanks." She sounded both surprised and pleased. She walked quickly to the service counter. The line wasn't long. She was back at the booth in a few minutes, carrying a bag of french fries and a soda. She slid into the seat opposite me. She smiled at me, and then she began to pop the fries into her mouth, one after the other. She had a small, pretty mouth, and when she opened it, it made a neat, round O. I had never noticed it before.

After a while, I asked her a question. "What do you do at Young Judaea?"

"We learn about Zionism, Jewish history, stuff like that," Abby replied. That must have been the most boring club in the world. My face must have registered my opinion, because she added quickly, "It's not like Hebrew School. It's fun. It's games, and songs, and dancing. And then we have these conventions and dances with clubs from all over the state. We get to meet a lot of different kids."

"Still sounds too much like Hebrew School to me," I said. "But, of course, you like Hebrew School."

Abby drew back, as if insulted. "What makes you think I like Hebrew School? I *hate* Hebrew School. I hate it this year, anyway."

"But you're always raising your hand," I said. "You're always answering questions."

"I have to do something to pass the time," she replied.

"I can think of other things."

"You mean like getting Mr. Hyman's goat." She took the words right out of my mouth. "That's too easy."

"Well, it doesn't matter anymore, anyway," I said. "They threw me out of the class."

"That's too bad," she said.

"Too bad? *I'm* glad."

"You can't have a bar mitzvah if you don't go to

Hebrew School. Don't you want to have a bar mitzvah?"

"No, I don't," I replied firmly, shaking my head. "That's a lot of crap. The whole thing is a lot of crap."

"What whole thing?" Abby asked. She sounded really interested.

"The whole being Jewish thing."

"You want to convert to something else?"

"Of course not." Now *I* was insulted. "I mean, I'm Jewish. I certainly don't want to get involved with any other religion."

"Being Jewish is not only a religion," Abby said slowly. "It's more complicated than that."

"Maybe that's the trouble," I responded. "It all takes so much time. I just want to do plain American things after school—you know, play football and basketball and all that stuff."

"Well, I think you can be a plain American and still be a Jew," she said.

"Well, I didn't say you couldn't," I retorted. I was getting confused.

Fortunately, Abby took off in a different direction. "I like being Jewish," she said. "I know the Jews have suffered a lot and all that. They still do, in lots of places. But I like being Jewish anyway."

I quoted something Bart always said whenever he and someone else agreed to disagree. "So, that's what makes horse races."

But Abby apparently wasn't ready to drop the subject. "Why don't you come to our Young Judaea party tomorrow?" she asked. "You might have fun."

I shook my head. If the other guys in the gang found out I'd been at a Young Judaea party, they'd laugh me out of town. I didn't have the slightest desire to go, anyway. "No, thanks. I've got other things to do."

Abby didn't take offense. She hadn't really expected me to accept her invitation. She pushed her bag of french fries toward me. "You want some?" she asked.

I'd eaten enough fries to hold me for that day at least, but I took a couple just to be polite. "Thanks," I said.

"I'll invite you to my bat mitzvah, anyway," Abby said. "I'll invite you even if you're not in Hebrew School anymore. My mother said I could invite all the kids in the class. She doesn't have to know you got thrown out." Suddenly a frown creased her forehead. "You will come, won't you? Just because you don't want a bar mitzvah yourself doesn't mean you won't go to other people's, does it?"

"Of course not," I replied. "Morty and Howie and those guys are friends of mine. I have to go to their bar mitzvahs. Will they invite everyone in the class too, do you think? Is that the way it's done?"

"I don't know if it'll be that way in our class," Abby said. "Every class is different. But it was that way in Laura and Kenny's classes." Laura and Kenny were Abby's older sister and brother. "I hope it's that way in our class, too," she added. "I think it's nice. Their classes were real groups. They had lots of fun together. Laura went to twenty-two parties the year she was thirteen, and Kenny went to twenty-six. He really threw those four extra parties up to her," she concluded with a laugh.

"Twenty-six?" I couldn't believe it. "Twenty-six? We don't have anything like twenty-six kids in our class. There're only about fifteen."

"Yeah, but you know," Abby explained, "you have a couple of friends from camp in another town, or a cousin or something. You're bound to get invited to a few from the Tuesday-Thursday class, too. It can come to twenty-six easy, for someone like Kenny, who's popular. I'm not popular, so I won't get invited to that many. But you are. You may get invited to more. You may get invited to thirty!"

"I don't think I'll go to all of them." I was not pleased by the prospect of thirty Friday nights and Saturdays spent in the synagogue. "I've been to my cousins'. They're boring. The services are so long, and all your old aunts and uncles look you over and pinch your cheeks. Then the dumb band plays all these silly games, and they expect you to get up and dance with the girls. That's not for me."

"Well, it's different when it's your own friend up there on the bimah chanting the haftarah," Abby said, "someone you know really well. I thought Laura's and Kenny's were really exciting. And the party's fun when you know the kids. I'm looking forward to the whole thing—even though I know no one will ask me to dance," she added, a touch mournfully.

"Why not?"

"I told you, I'm not popular."

I couldn't contradict her. She wasn't.

"But no one has to ask you for the game dances," she added, brightening. "You can just get up and do them."

I was thinking of something else. "Twenty-six presents," I moaned. "Twenty-six. How could your folks afford it?"

"Well, you kind of get it back, you know. After all, when those kids come to your bar mitzvah, they have to bring you a gift."

I hadn't thought of that.

Abby picked up her soda cup and drained the last drop. "Well," she said, gathering her packages together, "I've got to go now. Thanks for helping me."

"You having games at that Israeli cafe you're running tomorrow?" I asked. "Games with prizes?"

She nodded.

I reached into my pocket and pulled out the pair of mice from Woolworth's. "Here's something you can use for a prize. They haven't been touched. See? The price tag's still on them."

"Thanks, Vic," Abby said, sounding a little puzzled. But she took the tiny animals that I held out to her in the palm of my hand. "Young Judaea sure appreciates this." She didn't ask me how I came to be carrying two brand-new, unwrapped mice around in my coat pocket. "Well, so long. See you in school."

"So long," I echoed. I would see her in school. I always did. We ate lunch the same period. But would I say hello to her? I never had. Now I guessed I'd have to. Well, that was all right. I could afford to say hello to her. It was only the borderline kids who had to be careful about who they spoke to.

CHAPTER FIVE |

Monday afternoon, my mother picked me up after school. When we arrived at the temple, I couldn't see my father's yellow Cutlass parked anywhere in the lot. I wasn't surprised. I'd known Pop would be late. He'd complained about having to come at all because it meant leaving work early. He'd wanted the rabbi to make the meeting the next Sunday, but Mom was spending the weekend at a resort with some friends. The rabbi didn't want to wait until the Sunday after that. He wanted to get the matter settled. So Pop had agreed, reluctantly, to leave his office early. It was either that or meet with the rabbi at eleven o'clock at night, after he'd attended his meetings or taught his adult education classes, and Mom wouldn't consent to that.

Mom and I walked into the building. She looked

around the lobby curiously. "The place hasn't changed much since I was last here," she said. She and Bart never came to services, not even on the high holy days. She hadn't been inside since she'd left Pop. "You'd think in all this time they could have repaired the sign."

I followed her pointing finger. The letters above the door spelled out, in Hebrew and English, "Temple Brit Israel," but the B in "Brit" had fallen on its side. I'd never noticed that before.

We entered the rabbi's outer office. "Sit down, please, Vic, Mrs. Abrams . . ." Mrs. Kadin said, looking up from her typewriter.

"Mrs. Levine," Mom corrected quickly.

"Of course, Mrs. Levine," Mrs. Kadin said, blinking several times in embarrassment. "I'm sorry. I don't know how I could have made such a mistake."

It seemed to me a perfectly natural mistake. "It's no big deal," I murmured.

Mom didn't say anything.

"The rabbi will be with you in a couple of minutes," Mrs. Kadin said. "He has someone else with him now —an emergency."

I took the same black chair I'd sat in the last time I'd been in this office. Mom sat down on the sofa opposite me and picked up one of the magazines. She flipped through it idly and then, with a disgusted look, tossed it back on the table.

The door opened and my father came in. "Hi, Pop," I said.

"Hello, Vic." He sat down on the other black chair. "Hello, Millie," he added tentatively.

"Hello, Seymour," Mom replied in a subdued tone.

"Where's the rabbi?" Pop asked. "I thought we were supposed to be meeting with him."

"He's busy," I explained. "He has an emergency."

"I'm busy, too," Pop complained. "He should have had the courtesy to call me and let me know he'd be late. I wouldn't have had to leave the office so early."

"Oh, Seymour, don't make a federal case out of it," Mom said. "He'll be ready for us in a couple of minutes."

"Just because you have nothing more important to do doesn't mean my time isn't valuable," Pop retorted. "Time is money, you know."

"Seymour, if I hear that worn-out cliché once more in my life, I will personally strangle you," Mom replied, her voice low and angry.

It was beginning already. "Geezus, Mom, Pop," I interrupted, "you've been together two seconds and already you're fighting. Can't you cool it for a little while?"

They both leaned back in their seats. "Sorry, Vic," Mom said with a sigh. Pop picked up the magazine that Mom had discarded a few minutes before. His eyes seemed to move down the page. Perhaps he was actually reading it.

The door to the rabbi's study opened. A boy and a girl, neither more than nine years old, walked out, heads lowered, eyes puffy, as if they'd been crying. What could they possibly have done, at their age, to warrant a private emergency session with the rabbi? And what could the rabbi have said to make them so unhappy? I'd never know—and, of course, I didn't really care.

Rabbi Auerbach stood in the doorway. "Come in, please," he said. The three of us rose and entered the rabbi's study. He gestured to three chairs grouped in front of his desk. I sat facing him; Mom and Pop were on either side of me.

Pop didn't waste any time. "As I told you over the phone, Rabbi, I don't really see the point to this meeting. Frankly, I resent having to leave my office early on a very busy day in order to discuss a matter that is settled."

"Vic doesn't seem to understand that it's settled," Rabbi Auerbach replied mildly. "Vic tells me he won't come to me for instruction and he won't be bar mitzvahed. Isn't that what you said, Vic?"

"Yes," I replied firmly. "That's what I said."

"Vic has no choice in this matter," Pop announced. "I told you that over the phone. I'll punish him for misbehaving in Mr. Hyman's class. I'll cut his allowance in half for the next month. If I hear from you that he's not reporting to you as scheduled, I'll stop his allowance entirely."

"That seems a little extreme, Seymour," Mom said sharply.

Pop's hand clenched the edge of his chair. "Really, Millie," he said, "I don't know what this has to do with you. You don't support Vic. I do. You don't give him his allowance. I do." He turned and looked at the rabbi. "To tell you the truth, Rabbi, I don't know why she's here. She hardly ever sees Vic."

"That isn't true," Mom protested. "I see him every minute I can. I make a very special effort to see him."

"He told me," Pop retorted. "He told me you weren't really home very much this weekend. He told me he was alone in the house almost the whole weekend. He didn't even know he was telling me, but I got it out of him."

I leaned back in my seat. Usually I wanted to run from the room and hide my head under a pillow when Mom and Pop engaged in this kind of conversation. In the outer office I'd put a stop to it. But not now. Now I wanted it to play itself right into an impasse between the two of them.

"If you take away his allowance, I'll replace it," Mom shot back. "He needs his allowance. He needs it to buy dinner at McDonald's because you don't have any real food in the house."

"He lives with me, Millie." Pop bit off the end of each word as he spoke it. "I can't have you undermining my discipline. You're talking nonsense. You know perfectly well I'm not going to let him starve."

"Seymour, Millie," Rabbi Auerbach interrupted loudly, "I think you've gotten off the subject. We're supposed to be talking about Vic's bar mitzvah."

Pop turned to the rabbi, his hands spread out in a gesture of appeal. "But that's what we *are* talking about, Rabbi," he said. "She wants to take away the one weapon I have to make Vic do what we both agreed he should do. That was one thing we absolutely agreed upon. We absolutely agreed he should continue his Jewish education and be bar mitzvahed. Afterwards, he should go to Hebrew High School, too."

"Oh, my God," I groaned. This was the first time Pop had mentioned Hebrew High School.

Pop heard me. "But we can talk about that later," he added hastily. "It's the bar mitzvah I'm concerned about right now."

"Yes," Rabbi Auerbach agreed.

"She consented to it." Pop jerked his head in Mom's direction.

"Of course I did," Mom replied, a pained expression on her face. "I still agree to it. When did I say I didn't?"

"You're going to make it impossible for me to enforce his coming here," Pop replied, his voice full of venom. "So that's the same thing as going back on your agreement."

I dug my fingernails into my palms. They sounded like a pair of five-year-olds shouting bathroom words at each other. Even if it was serving my ends, I was embarrassed by it in front of the rabbi. The rabbi didn't seem upset, though. His deep brown eyes glanced sharply from one of them to the other; his lined, tired face was calm. I guess he had seen just about everything. Nothing my mother or father said was going to surprise him.

"I think eating properly is more important than a bar mitzvah," Mom said. "Even the rabbi would agree to that, wouldn't you, Rabbi?"

But Rabbi Auerbach was too smart to answer.

Mom went on talking directly to the rabbi. "I agreed to the bar mitzvah because I think it's important for a child to be brought up in a religion. I've always thought so. And I agreed to it because it was important to Seymour. It really mattered to him. I'm not an unreasonable person. I supported the idea of the bar mitzvah, even though, of course, it doesn't really matter to me, not being Jewish myself."

Rabbi Auerbach's face went white. He leaned forward in his chair. "Millie," he asked quietly, "would you please say that again?"

"I support the idea of a bar mitzvah," she repeated.

"No. What you said after that."

My father had risen from his seat as suddenly as if he'd been bitten by a big green fly. Now he was standing behind my mother's chair. He put his hands on her shoulders. "Millie didn't say anything else, Rabbi. She supports the idea of a bar mitzvah. That's all she said. She said it several times."

My mother brushed my father's hands off her shoulders and turned so that she could look at him, her face creased by a puzzled frown.

"She did say something else, Seymour," Rabbi Auerbach contradicted. "She said she isn't Jewish. Millie, Seymour, is that true?"

My father's whole body slumped. His hands hung down at his sides like two hunks of meat. "Cripes, Millie," he groaned, "don't you know when to keep your mouth shut?"

"I don't know what you're talking about, Seymour," she snapped. "I think you've gone crazy."

"That's nothing new." He walked back to his chair and collapsed into it with a thump. "The fat's in the fire now," he grumbled.

"Millie," Rabbi Auerbach said quietly, "are you Jewish?"

Pop raised his hand and then, giving up, lowered it.

"No, Rabbi Auerbach, I'm not," my mother replied mildly. She sounded more than a little mystified. "I'm not really anything. My parents weren't at all religious. I don't think I was even baptized."

"But they weren't Jewish," Rabbi Auerbach said.

"Oh, no."

"You're sure of that?"

Mom laughed. "Of course, I'm sure. In the little Pennsylvania mining town where I grew up, there was no such thing as a Jew. I never even saw a Jew until I went to college, except in the movies or on TV. After my parents were killed in an automobile accident, I moved to the city, and then of course I met plenty of Jews. I even married two of them. I even have a Jewish son," she added, smiling.

"No, Millie." Rabbi Auerbach shook his head. "I'm afraid you don't. I suppose I should have inquired about this sooner, and I suppose I should find a better way of saying it. But I don't know any better way. Millie, you don't have a Jewish son."

Now it was my turn to feel all the blood drain from my face. "What do you mean?" I asked. The expression on Pop's face could have turned the rabbi to stone.

But Rabbi Auerbach wasn't looking at Pop. He was looking at me. "The definition of *Jew* is very simple," he said quietly. "It has nothing to do with the desire to be Jewish or the level of Jewish observance. A Jew is a person born of a Jewish mother. That's all there is to it.

Unless you convert, of course." His face lightened a little. "Millie, did you ever go through the process of conversion?" he asked hopefully.

Mom shook her head. "No," she said. "Seymour and I were married in the city by a justice of the peace. A justice of the peace married Bart and me, too. I'm not a Jew, and I never have been. But I don't see what that has to do with Seymour's Jewishness, or Vic's."

"Nothing to do with Seymour's," Rabbi Auerbach explained, "but everything to do with Vic's."

"Are you telling me that I'm not a Jew?" I asked softly.

The rabbi nodded slowly. "Yes," he said. "That's what I'm telling you."

"That's ridiculous," I objected. What he was saying didn't make any sense to me.

"Why?" Rabbi Auerbach asked mildly, looking directly at me. "It settles the bar mitzvah question."

"It's not important" Pop interjected. "You could ignore it."

The rabbi turned to him. "I'm sorry, Seymour," he said, "I can't bar mitzvah a boy who isn't Jewish. That should be obvious to you."

"But five minutes ago you would have bar mitzvahed him," Pop protested.

"Five minutes ago I didn't know he wasn't Jewish," the rabbi explained. "It's not my custom to check the ancestry of every member of the congregation. But when it's brought directly to my attention, as in this case, I have no choice. Judaism is a religion of law, Seymour. I have to follow the law."

"But I've always been Jewish," I cried out suddenly. "If I'm not Jewish, what am I?"

"You're Victor Abrams, a very bright, very able young man," the rabbi said.

I shook my head. That wasn't true. I was Victor Abrams, troublemaker. The rabbi was just trying to butter me up.

"You, of course, knew that Millie wasn't Jewish when you married her," Rabbi Auerbach said to Pop.

Pop nodded. "But she agreed from the first day that if we had any kids, they should be raised Jewish. She said it didn't matter to her."

Rabbi Auerbach turned next to me. "Did you realize, Vic? Did you realize that your mother wasn't Jewish?"

I rubbed my forehead and tried to consider the question objectively. "She always put up a little tree in the living room at Christmas," I recalled, speaking slowly. "I never thought anything of it. There are other Jewish kids who have Christmas trees."

The rabbi nodded, his face grim.

"I guess I knew she wasn't Jewish. I must have," I went on. "But it wasn't anything I ever thought about." Mom didn't have any relatives, and most of her friends were Jewish. Even Bart was Jewish. So I really never had thought about it. I had never considered it. I remembered the day we'd all tapped our pencils in Mr. Hyman's class. "Even when Mr. Hyman told us that a Jew was a person born of a Jewish mother, I didn't think about it," I added. "I never thought what he said had anything to do with me."

"I'm afraid it does," the rabbi said. "But it's OK. Now

you're free. Now you don't have to come to Hebrew School. You don't have to have a bar mitzvah. Even your father can't insist on it. Even I can't make you." He smiled. "You must feel glad about that, Vic."

"Well, yeah, sure," I replied. "But it *is* a shock. All your life you have one idea of yourself, and then all of a sudden you find out it isn't true. I don't see how that can be. It seems wrong to me."

"Judaism is built around law," the rabbi said. "I think you understand that. We have no creed of belief that Jews must adhere to. What we have are laws."

"But people break the laws all the time," I pointed out. "My father doesn't keep a kosher home. Neither does my grandmother. Still, they're Jewish."

Rabbi Auerbach nodded. "Yes, they're Jewish. You can break every law in the Torah and the Talmud, including the one that says, 'Thou shalt not kill,' and still be a Jew. It's what I said before. A Jew isn't defined by his level of observance, or by his morality, or by his desire to be a Jew. A *good* Jew may be, but not a Jew, just as a good human being is defined by his behavior, but a human being in general is not. A Jew is defined as a Jew because his mother was Jewish." The rabbi glanced from my mother to my father. "Now, try to understand my position," he said. "I'm a Conservative rabbi. I believe in the law. It's my job to uphold it. I can't change it to suit my own convenience. Knowing a woman isn't Jewish, I can no more participate in her son's bar mitzvah than I can knowingly eat a piece of pork or knowingly saw wood on the Sabbath."

"You're sitting here and telling me you won't bar

mitzvah my son?" Pop said, his voice rising in anger. "I never heard of such a thing. I'm going to resign from the temple."

"I'm sorry to hear you say that, Seymour," Rabbi Auerbach said.

"Though not surprised," Mom added dryly.

Rabbi Auerbach ignored that remark. "But I can't rewrite the Torah," he said to my father. "I can't rewrite Jewish law to suit each congregant."

"You can interpret it," Pop said. "That's your job."

"Yes," Rabbi Auerbach agreed, "but this law allows for no interpretation. It's perfectly and absolutely clear. On some issues in Jewish law, rabbis and scholars had different opinions. It's possible to pick and choose among interpretations to find the one that best suits a particular occasion. That isn't the case here. There's no disagreement in the tradition."

"Of course," Mom said slowly, "Vic could convert. Just as I could have converted, he could convert."

Rabbi Auerbach nodded. "That's perfectly true, Millie. Vic could convert. Then, of course, I'd be very happy to bar mitzvah him. Nothing would give me greater pleasure. But he doesn't want to be bar mitzvahed. He wants to be free of the whole business." The rabbi turned to me. "Don't you, Vic?" he asked, his eyes directly on my face.

"Yes," I said. "I want to be free of the whole business." I was surprised that I didn't experience an enormous feeling of relief as I said those words.

"What about a conversion?" Pop asked as if he hadn't even heard me. "What would Vic have to do to convert? It shouldn't be too difficult." He sounded excited by the idea.

"Well," the rabbi replied, "the first part *is* easy. If Vic were an adult, he'd have to study. But that's not required of a small child, let's say a non-Jewish child who's being adopted by Jewish parents. It's expected that such a child will learn what he or she has to know from being brought up in a Jewish home and getting normal religious training, like any other Jewish child. Well, Vic's not a small child, but he's been enrolled in Hebrew School for three years, and he's been brought up in a Jewish home . . ." Here the rabbi hesitated briefly. Then he pushed on. "So the education part is taken care of. So what he'd have to do is go to the mikvah—"

"Mikvah?" Mom queried.

"Ritual bath," I explained. "Like a little swimming pool." I remembered that from Mrs. Rifkind's class. It was surprising the things that were coming back to me today. "That's nothing," I added.

The rabbi rubbed his chin. "The last part isn't so nothing," he said. For the first time that afternoon I caught a note of real discomfort in his voice. He turned to my mother. "Was Vic circumcised at birth?" he asked.

"Of course," she said. "Right in the hospital, just a few hours after he was born. The pediatrician did it. He asked me if I wanted a brit. He thought I was Jewish, too," she added with a small laugh. "With a name like Abrams, that's an easy assumption to make. But I told him no brit. A brit is barbaric, I think. But if he'd had one, he'd have been Jewish now, right?"

Sadly, the rabbi shook his head. "No," he said. "I guess you don't understand. Brit or no brit when he was born, if Vic wanted to be a Jew today, he'd have to submit to a hatafat dam brit—a symbolic circumcision."

"A symbolic circumcision?" Pop didn't sound so excited anymore.

"Since he's already been circumcised, it wouldn't be such a big thing," Rabbi Auerbach said lightly. "We'd just have to draw a symbolic drop of blood."

I shivered a little. "From where?"

Of course I knew the answer before I heard Rabbi Auerbach reply quietly, "From the end of the penis."

"Barbaric!" Mom cried. "Absolutely barbaric. I won't allow it. Seymour," she shouted angrily, "how can you even contemplate making him go through such a thing?"

"I'm not, I'm not," Pop replied quickly. "Of course I'm not. I wouldn't dream of permitting it."

"Well . . . it would be up to me," I said quietly.

"Yes, I guess so. Anyway," he added with a wave of his hand, "the question is academic."

I turned to the rabbi. "Does it hurt?"

"If you had to endure a full circumcision at your age, it would hurt like blazes," he said. "Not the operation itself—that would be done under anesthetic—but the aftermath. You don't need a full circumcision, though. A symbolic cut oughtn't to hurt more than a splinter. I think the idea of it is much more upsetting than the actuality."

"Upsetting? It's barbaric, it's medieval!" It was obvious that no matter what Rabbi Auerbach said, Mom wasn't going to change her opinion about symbolic circumcisions. She turned to me. "You wanted to be out of it," she said, "and now you *are* out of it. I think you're pretty lucky. You should be jumping for joy."

"I'm afraid I have to agree with Millie," Pop said stiffly. "The whole idea is obnoxious. I couldn't ask Vic to have anything to do with it." He turned and stared at me. "Isn't it funny?" His voice was calm. "You win, Vic."

Mom stood up. "Are you going home, Seymour," she asked, "or should I drop Vic?"

"I'm going home." He, too, rose from his seat. "It's much too late to try to go back to the office. Come on, Vic."

"If you need me," Rabbi Auerbach said to me, "just call—any time. Or drop by. I'll tell Mrs. Kadin you have priority."

What made him think I'd need him? But all I said was "OK. Thanks."

I was free of Hebrew School. I was free of bar mitzvahs. I was free of all of it, and my father couldn't do anything about it. Like Mom had said, I should have been jumping for joy. But I wasn't. Not that I felt bad or anything. I simply felt odd, as if I were a balloon some kid had just let go of.

CHAPTER SIX |

"So you're not a Jew," Morty said. "Congratulations."

"I still feel like a Jew," I said.

"So what does a Jew feel like?" Howie asked. "Does a Jew feel any different from anyone else?" Howie answered his own question. "Maybe a Jew has some different ideas about some things, but he doesn't *feel* any different."

We were standing in the hall before the bell rang for homeroom. We'd hung our jackets in our lockers and taken out the books we'd need for the first half of the day. We were leaning against the locker doors, as we always did, but instead of coolly staring at the passing parade and mouthing off an occasional smart remark, we were engrossed in a serious discussion.

"No more Hebrew School," Morty said. "You were just born lucky. Everything always works out for you."

I couldn't believe my ears. Morty's parents lived under the same roof, apparently quite contentedly. My folks did not. Well, Mom and Dad had worked hard to convince me it was better for all of us this way, and I was used to it now, anyway. I mean, after all, in this day and age I'm hardly the only one. But lucky would have been if it hadn't had to happen in the first place. "I'm no luckier than you," I said, "or Howie." Howie was more to the point. His parents had just separated a month before. He was still hoping they'd work things out. I'd told him not to count on it. I had even given him the old it-may-be-better-this-way routine. And, of course, it may be.

"You're sure luckier than me," Howie said. "I still have to go to Hebrew School. I still have to have a bar mitzvah."

"It's my choice," I said. "I could convert."

"But you won't," Morty said. "You're out of it. You're right where you want to be."

"Yeah," I agreed. "That's right." What Morty said was true. I was right where I wanted to be.

"So why are you frowning?" Morty asked. "You look like you just lost your last friend."

"I'm not frowning," I replied. "I'm just thinking."

"I thought I smelled something burning," Howie chimed in. His sense of humor had never developed past the fifth grade.

"Listen," I said, "you guys will still invite me to your bar mitzvahs, won't you? Even if I'm not having one?"

"What a stupid question," Morty said. "Of course we

will. I'm inviting Pat and Big John, and they're certainly not having bar mitzvahs."

"Yeah, me too," Howie said. Howie wasn't actually part of the gang, but he would have liked to be.

"And Stewie?" I asked. "Are you inviting Stewie?"

"I'm thinking about it," Morty said. "I don't know. My bar mitzvah isn't until December. I'll see what happens in the next couple of months."

"You should invite him," I said. "The gang has to stick together."

"I'll see what happens," Morty repeated.

The bell rang then. Howie walked quickly toward his homeroom. Morty and I sauntered into ours. Stewie was already there, talking to Debbie Barton. But when he saw us, he took his seat behind me. Morty was next to him. "Did you hear?" Morty whispered. "Did you hear about Vic?"

Stewie punched my shoulder. "What about you? They finally caught up to you, huh? They know about the bank heist. I told you to watch out. Now you're in for it."

"Can't you shut up for two minutes, Stewie?" Morty complained. "Listen to me. Vic doesn't have to go to Hebrew School anymore. He can play Space Invaders and Galaxia every day of the week if he wants to."

"Hey, that's great!" Stewie exclaimed. "You finally got to your father, huh?"

I didn't say anything. I let Morty talk for me. "No, it's not that. The rabbi won't let him have a bar mitzvah. He found out yesterday that Vic's mother isn't Jewish.

If your mother isn't Jewish, then you're not Jewish."

"This gets better every minute." For a split second, I thought Stewie was going to kiss me, but he managed to restrain himself and merely punched my shoulder again. "I always knew a tough guy like you couldn't really be . . ." He looked from me to Morty and shut his mouth. Morty stared back for a moment and then turned away. I had a feeling Stewie had just killed his last chance at an invitation to Morty's bar mitzvah. "I didn't mean anything," Stewie said. "Everyone knows you kikes aren't famous for courage."

"Knock it off, Stewie," I said.

"Boy." Stewie's eyes were on me now. "What's the matter with you? Now that *kike* doesn't apply to you, suddenly you get sensitive about it. You're nuts."

"Cripes, Stewie," I said, "if you don't understand, I can't explain. There are all kinds of ways of using a word. Different people can mean different things when they say it."

Stewie frowned in puzzlement. He really didn't know what I was talking about. "I'll tell you what I don't understand," he said. "I don't understand that rule about your mother. Your father's Jewish. You were brought up Jewish."

I sighed. How could I possibly explain it? I hardly understood it myself. "Being Jewish isn't just a religion," I began. "There are Jews who don't believe anything and don't practice anything. They're still Jews. So who is Jewish? The rabbis and sages said you're Jewish if your mother is Jewish. That's all."

"Well," Stewie said magnanimously, "what difference does it make, anyway? The important thing is that you're out of it."

"It's OK to be Jewish," I said. "I never minded that. It's the services and the school and the bar mitzvah stuff I'm glad to be out of. That's what's important."

Stewie nodded. "Whatever you say, boy. Whatever you say."

By the end of the morning Big John and Pat and four guys from the Hebrew School class had all expressed their opinion on the subject. It was unanimous. Everyone congratulated me. Pat and Big John were glad because I'd have time now to do the things I liked doing. The boys from Hebrew School agreed with Morty and Howie. I'd been born lucky, they said. They were all going right home after school to check out their mothers' ancestries. They didn't have much hope, though. "Not with my grandmother's Yiddish accent," Ira Shapiro said sadly.

I was late getting to lunch. Mrs. Dafter sent me and Paul Orlando to the book room to return thirty-two copies of *The Old Man and the Sea* and to pick up thirty-two copies of the grammar book. Why she had to wait till the very end of the period to send us on such an errand, I don't know. I almost told her it was too close to lunch to go. We only had half an hour for lunch as it was. If you bought your lunch, as I did, your actual eating time ran to about thirteen minutes. I was lucky I didn't have an ulcer.

But then I decided I didn't care if I missed part of lunch. I knew that today I would be the main topic of lunch table conversation whether I was there or not, and I'd just as soon miss some of it.

By the time we'd lugged the grammar books back to Mrs. Dafter, lunch period was half over. I ran down to the cafeteria to grab a couple of ice cream sandwiches. I'd be able to do that quickly because by this time there'd be no line. I'd be able to eat them quickly, too.

I picked up the sandwiches, paid for them, and walked out into the lunchroom. I paused for a moment to survey the scene. Waves of noise ebbed and flowed around me. Everywhere, kids were moving around—sitting down, standing up, scraping chairs against the floor, throwing wads of garbage into pails, running to say something to someone at another table, tossing apple cores at each other. The teachers on cafeteria duty tried to prevent flagrant littering, food fights, and screaming, but how could a mere two adults really tell who'd spilled the full milk carton on the floor or who'd shouted the big F in a room full of three hundred kids? If you avoided the tables near where the monitors stood, you could pretty well do what you wanted in the lunchroom.

I moved toward our table, in the middle of the room. Pat, Big John, and Stewie were in their usual seats. A friend of Stewie's, Arnold Johnstone, was sitting in Morty's seat. Morty was nowhere to be seen.

Something was going on. Stewie and Arnold were throwing something, something small, and laughing hysterically with each toss. As I drew closer, I could see that they were throwing pennies. And they weren't playing matching games, either. You don't have to toss the pennies to do that. Besides, no one plays with pennies. It's not worth it. It's hardly worth it, nowadays, to play with quarters.

What Stewie and Arnold were doing was throwing the pennies at Abby Greenglass. She sat two tables away with three of her friends. She probably sat there every day. I'd never noticed that before. One of her friends was a real grind named Sally Mason. I didn't even know the names of the other two.

Sally and the other girls were shrieking at Stewie and Arnold to stop. But Abby wasn't shrieking. She didn't even glance in Stewie and Arnold's direction. She just sat there, looking down at her tray and munching on a sandwich, while the pennies clattered on the floor and the table around her. A couple of them actually landed in her lap.

I got to our table just in time to hear Arnold call out, "All right, money lover. Pick up the pennies, money lover."

"Jews pick up pennies," Stewie chanted. "Jews pick up pennies, Jews pick up pennies."

Big John saw me coming. "Hey, guys . . ." he began, but he was too late. I slammed my books down on the table. Arnold and Stewie turned their heads sharply. They saw me, too.

"What the hell are you guys doing?" I shouted.

Stewie wasn't even embarrassed. "You want to help us? You have to use your own pennies."

I walked around to his side of the table, grabbed him by the collar, and pulled him up out of his seat.

"What's the matter with you?" he whined. "You aren't even Jewish anymore. What do you care?"

Blood rushed to my head. I was so enraged I couldn't see. I pulled back my fist, thrust it forward, and hit Stewie in the jaw with such force that he screamed. His cry rose above the lunchroom clamor like the screech of an owl in the middle of the night. Before I could hit him again, Big John was behind me, pulling me away. "Save it," Big John ordered. "Save it for later."

But he was too late again. Mr. Stanhope had heard Stewie's scream. When he got to our table, he could see a thin streak of blood trickling out the side of Stewie's mouth. "What's going on here?" Mr. Stanhope asked, his eyes blazing with fury.

"He hit me," Stewie moaned, pointing.

"He was calling people names," I said.

"You?" Mr. Stanhope asked.

"Girls," I said. "He was throwing pennies at girls."

The fury faded from Mr. Stanhope's face, to be replaced by curiosity. "What girls?" he asked.

I didn't say anything. Neither did Stewie. "Abby Greenglass," Arnold supplied helpfully. Arnold was very dumb.

By this time Abby was sipping her chocolate milk. "Come here, Abby," Mr. Stanhope called to her. She walked slowly over to our table. "Were these boys throwing pennies at you?" Mr. Stanhope asked.

Abby, her lips pressed together, nodded slowly.

"Why?"

Abby shrugged.

"There must have been a reason," Mr. Stanhope said. He wasn't too smart, either.

"Ask them," Abby snapped.

Mr. Stanhope turned to Stewie. "Why were you throwing pennies at Abby?" he asked.

"We were giving them to her," Stewie said. "She collects them."

"If you want to give someone pennies," Mr. Stanhope said, "you don't throw them. You hand them to her. One day's detention for you Stewie, and one day for you, Arnold. Arnold, you pick up those pennies. If they mean so little to you, you can put them in the heart fund box. Stewie, get over to the nurse and have her look at that jaw. John, you go with him." He took a pad of passes out of his pocket and hastily scribbled two for them. Stewie held his hand to his jaw as he followed Big John out of the lunchroom.

Then Mr. Stanhope returned his attention to me. "As for you, my fine friend," he said, "there is no excuse for brawling in the school building. You know the rules. It was very chivalrous of you to come to Abby's defense." His tone was heavy with irony. "But you certainly went about it the wrong way. We don't tolerate hitting, not in any form, or for any reason. Three days' detention for you, my friend. By rights, I should give you a week. You're getting away with murder." He paused for a moment, and then he added, "But then, you always do, don't you?" He shook his head and walked away, leaving me and Abby standing there, looking at each other.

The bell rang. Abby and I were swept along by the hordes of kids flowing out of the lunchroom. We moved down the corridor next to each other, I munching an ice cream sandwich, almost as horrendous an infraction of the rules as hitting Stewie.

"I saw you hit him," Abby said quietly. "You didn't have to do that. He doesn't bother me."

"He bothers me," I said. "Anyway, why were you just taking it?" I was angry at her, too. "Why weren't you yelling at him?"

"What's the point?" she replied reasonably. "If I yell at him, he's happy. He wants to get my goat. That's why he does it. Well, I won't give him the satisfaction."

"You mean this isn't the first time?" I asked, amazed.

"Of course not. Stewie throws pennies at me every chance he gets."

"There ought to be something you can do about it," I said. I'm not the type who takes insults lying down.

"Like hitting him?" she responded with a light laugh.

"Maybe you ought to talk to Dr. Hathaway." He was the principal. I'd never thought I'd live to suggest that a person voluntarily enter the enemy camp.

Abby shrugged. "Stewie's going to think what he thinks, no matter what I do. He's just an anti-Semite, that's all."

Stewie the anti-Semite. I'd never thought of him in that way before. Anti-Semites were people who painted swastikas on synagogue walls or knocked down gravestones in Jewish cemeteries or burned crosses on the lawns of Jewish homes—or burned six million Jews in ovens. They weren't people I knew. But I had to admit that Stewie was showing some qualifications for the title. He'd never really demonstrated them before, at least not to me. But I guess in his mind I had been different. I had been a Jew who was OK. And now I wasn't a Jew at all. "What gets me," I said, "is that it doesn't seem to bother you."

"Oh, it bothers me," Abby said. "I don't like it. But what am I supposed to do about it?"

"Next time," I urged, "tell Dr. Hathaway."

Abby laughed. "OK, if it'll make you happy. Anyway, now that Stewie knows how you feel, maybe there won't be a next time." We had come to the library. She stopped walking. "Here's where I go in," she said. I stopped walking, too. "I'm glad you care, really I am," she said softly. "I thought maybe you wouldn't, because you hated Hebrew School so much, and now you don't have to go anymore."

"Oh, so you heard," I said. "You heard I'm not Jewish."

She shook her head. "It sounds crazy to me," she said. She reached out and touched my arm briefly. "Anyway, whatever you are, I just want to say thanks. I mean it. Thanks for what you did." Before I could answer her, she wheeled around and disappeared through the doorway.

Three days' detention. Three whole days. Well, I had a lot to think about. Now I was sure of plenty of time in which to do the thinking.

CHAPTER SEVEN |

That night Abby called me up. "I told my mom what happened today," she said. "She feels terrible that you got into trouble on account of me."

"It wasn't on account of you," I assured her. "It was on account of Stewie."

"Well, that's what I told her," Abby replied matter-of-factly. "I said it wasn't me. I said you'd have done the same thing no matter who Stewie had been throwing pennies at."

"If Stewie had been throwing pennies just to throw them, I wouldn't have cared." I wanted to be perfectly honest. "It was the Jewish thing that got me."

"Yes, well, I know." Abby was apparently as eager to be perfectly honest as I was. "But she still thinks we owe you. She wants to say thanks."

"Oh, that's all right. She doesn't have to." I certainly

didn't want to get on the phone with Mrs. Greenglass. What could I possibly have to say to her? "Tell her it was nothing."

"I told her that already," Abby replied.

"You did?" She could have been a little more tactful. I was beginning to think Abby carried honesty to an unnecessary extreme.

Abby laughed. "Mom doesn't think it was nothing. She wants you to come to dinner Friday night, if you can."

"Is she a good cook?" I asked. If Abby could say whatever she felt like, so could I.

Abby didn't take offense. She just laughed again. "Yes, she's a good cook, and so am I, and so is my father. Dad and I do most of the dinner Friday night because she doesn't get home from work until after six." Abby's mother was a lawyer—Oppenheim and Greenglass was the name of her firm. I knew that because they had been Pop's lawyers on the divorce. Dr. Greenglass was a dean at the county college.

"What are you planning to serve Friday night?" I asked.

"For heaven's sake, Vic, it's only Tuesday," she giggled. "How do I know?"

"Well," I amended, "what kind of stuff do you usually have for dinner?"

"Friday night is special," she explained. "We usually have chicken or roast beef or brisket. And we have a noodle pudding, or a potato pudding, and a fresh vegetable, and something good for dessert. Mom bakes the dessert Thursday night."

"Maybe this Friday night you could try for roast beef," I suggested.

"OK," she agreed.

"I'll come," I said. I would now easily be able to avoid my grandmother's if Pop tried to drag me there. "What time?"

"About seven."

"OK."

"Well, so long, then."

"So long." After I'd hung up, I wondered if I'd done the right thing. I really didn't want to get too involved with Abby. I wasn't ready for girls yet, except for looking, and when I was ready, I certainly wouldn't pick one who still wore her hair in pigtails. Anyway, she wore her hair in pigtails some of the time. We rated girls on a scale of one to ten. If Debbie Barton was a ten, then Abby Greenglass was a two. She was a two on her good days. To tell the truth, we never even rated her. She never came up in that kind of discussion.

But I guess if you looked at her objectively, you'd have to admit Abby wasn't actually ugly. Besides, the dinner promised to be worth eating, and Abby didn't do anything more when she saw me in the halls at school over the next few days than duck her head in a sort of barely noticeable half-nod. I didn't see her after school anymore. She was at Hebrew School; I was serving detention.

So I never called her to wriggle out of the invitation. Promptly at seven on Friday, dressed in clean jeans and a long-sleeved turtleneck instead of my usual T-shirt, I presented myself at the Greenglasses' door.

Abby's older sister, Laura, let me in. "Hi, Vic," she said. "We're glad you could come." She led me into the living room. Abby wasn't there. Neither was her mother. But there was a crowd. I needn't have worried about what I was going to say to Abby's folks. In such a mob, they probably wouldn't even notice me. Laura's boyfriend, Todd, was there, and Dr. Greenglass's mother, and Mrs. Greenglass's sister, who was called Aunt Babs by everyone, and Kenny's buddy Mickey, who was staying for the whole week while his parents were on vacation, and Mickey's little brother, Richard, who seemed to be staying, too. The house wasn't large; I wondered where they were all bedding down. A few of them should have come over to our place, where a whole bedroom stood empty every night of the week, to say nothing of the studio couch in the family room.

Abby came in carrying a plate of chopped liver and some crackers. She passed them around while her father served the grown-ups cocktails and the kids soda or apple juice. When she got to me, she said, "Hi, Vic. I'm glad you could come. Did you meet everyone?"

"Yes," I said. "Your sister introduced me."

"Good." She moved on then, offering chopped liver to the others. Her mother followed, passing around a tray filled with sliced raw vegetables and a dip made of Russian dressing. I ate the chopped liver, but I skipped the vegetables. I was sitting next to Aunt Babs. Mostly she talked to Todd, on her other side. I didn't feel uncomfortable, though. Everyone was noisy and friendly, and kept pushing things to eat and drink on me.

After a while, Dr. Greenglass said it was time to go

into the dining room. On the sideboard two candles were burning. The tablecloth was gold, and in the middle of the table gold and white chrysanthemums were arranged in a crystal bowl. Embroidered linen covered the challah, and wine for Kiddush sat in a heavy, embossed silver cup at Dr. Greenglass's place. "Sit anywhere," he said to the crowd. "Just make sure, if you're a man, there's a yarmulke at your place." Each yarmulke was different. Mine was green velvet. When I picked it up I looked inside. Inscribed in gold letters were the words "Sanford Spector. Bar Mitzvah. February 25, 1978." Each yarmulke was a souvenir from a different occasion.

Abby sat down next to me. "We have roast beef," she said. "Just like you ordered."

"Hey, that's good!" I responded. It would make up for having to sit through prayers. At my grandmother's on Friday night we never had prayers, and, of course, at Mom's or Pop's we didn't even have Friday night.

But sitting through prayers didn't turn out to be so difficult, not in that house. There were a lot of people, and mostly they sang everything. Dr. Greenglass chanted Kiddush, the blessing over the wine. Before he did that, he said some other prayers. He translated them for the benefit of Mickey and Richard, who weren't Jewish. He was translating them for my benefit, too, even if he didn't know it. The first prayer was for Kenny. It asked, among other things, that he "grow to be like Ephraim and Manasseh." Then he blessed his daughters. He asked that they grow like Sarah, Rebecca, Rachel, and Leah. Then he made a prayer for his wife. He said she was a woman of valor and her price was above rubies. After all of that, he finally got to Kiddush. The rest of the family sang the last part along with him. Aunt Babs sang way off key, but that didn't stop her from singing very loud.

Mr. Greenglass asked Abby to recite the blessing over the challah, the braided Sabbath loaf. After that, we all took a sip of the wine and a bite of the bread. Then we had dinner. It was delicious. I didn't have much chance to talk to Abby while we were eating. She and Laura and Kenny kept popping up and down, serving the meal. Mostly, her mother and father stayed at the table.

Mrs. Greenglass brought in dessert, though, I guess because she had baked it and didn't want anyone to mess it up. It was a nut cake covered with a chocolate icing. It was probably the most delicious thing I'd ever eaten in my life. I didn't wolf it down. I let each bite linger on my tongue. I wanted to remember it forever.

"Is it good?" Mrs. Greenglass asked me anxiously. "Do you like it? It's a new recipe."

"Like it?" I exclaimed. "I love it. If I died now, I'd die happy."

Mrs. Greenglass grinned. "I'm really glad you came for supper, Vic," she said.

"So am I," I replied.

"We really appreciate what you did in the lunchroom that day," she added.

"I didn't do it for Abby, you know," I said.

She nodded. "Of course not. You'd have done it for anyone. We appreciate that, too. We're very disturbed by the recent rise in anti-Semitic incidents, and we're glad when someone takes a stand against them. It might have been better to speak to the boy, though," she suggested gently. "You really didn't have to hit him."

I said nothing. She didn't know Stewie. She didn't really know me, either.

"I don't want to sound as if I'm scolding you," she added. "You've been punished for hitting him. Abby told me that, too."

"One funny thing, Mrs. Greenglass," I said, "I was much more upset by the whole incident than Abby was."

"Well, she was more upset than she let you know," Mrs. Greenglass said. "It wasn't the first time it had happened, and she was beginning to get pretty annoyed."

"But she didn't cry or anything like that," I said. "I'd expect a girl to cry."

Mrs. Greenglass raised her eyebrows. "Would you?" she asked. "I think Abby feels good about her Jewishness," she continued thoughtfully. "All my children do, I hope. That gives them the strength not to be unduly upset by anti-Semitism. They know who they are, and they know what they're worth."

We didn't have a chance to talk any more just then. Dr. Greenglass was passing out little pamphlets containing the Birkat Hamazan, the grace after meals. It was much longer than any of the other prayers. It took us ten minutes to sing it through. The Greenglasses knew a lot of good tunes for different parts of it, though. They sang even louder than before, and Aunt Babs was even more off key. After that, we all sang a lot of other songs. Some of them I'd heard in Mrs. Rifkind's class, and some of them I hadn't. They were all pretty simple. Group singing wasn't exactly my thing, but the rest of the crowd kind of swept me along. Even Mickey and Richard were singing. When they didn't know the words, they just sang "la, la, la," or banged on the table with a spoon. I did the same.

After the singing, we all helped clear the table. Grandma Greenglass and Aunt Babs loaded the dishwasher. Kenny, Mickey, and Richard went upstairs to watch TV. Laura and Todd went out. For a little while I sat in the living room with Abby and Dr. and Mrs. Greenglass. This time Dr. Greenglass brought up Stewie and the pennies. Even in casual conversation, he talked like a professor. "It was especially interesting of you to do what you did," he said, "in light of the fact that you had just dropped out of Hebrew School."

"I didn't drop out," I said sharply. "The rabbi threw me out because he found out my mother isn't Jewish. I can't have a bar mitzvah unless I go through a conversion."

"I stand corrected," Dr. Greenglass said.

"And, of course, Vic isn't going to be converted," Abby said. "He never wanted to be in Hebrew School or have a bar mitzvah, anyway. He's happy to be out of it."

I frowned at her. Who'd given her permission to speak for me? I was getting tired of everyone's being so sure they knew what I was going to do. "I haven't made up my mind yet," I announced. "Maybe I will be converted." I had never before said that out loud. I had never even been aware of thinking it.

"And go to Hebrew School?" Mrs. Greenglass asked. "And have a bar mitzvah?"

"If I decide to do it," I said, "I'll do the whole thing."

"But you hate Hebrew School!" Abby exclaimed.

"You told me you hate it, too," I reminded her. "If your parents told you you could quit, would you?"

She shook her head. "I don't know. You get bad teachers sometimes, but that doesn't necessarily mean you quit. The same thing happens in regular school, and you don't quit."

"Well, it's not quite the same thing, darling," Mrs. Greenglass pointed out. "You couldn't quit regular school, even if your parents said it was all right. That's against the law."

"Oh, Mother, you know what I mean," Abby protested impatiently.

"No, Abby, we don't know what you mean," Dr. Greenglass said. "You have to *say* what you mean."

"Dad, don't be so fussy," Abby complained.

"Careless speech is a sign of careless thought," Dr. Greenglass intoned, as if he were lecturing a class at the college.

"All right, Father dear, I will explain it to you." Abby pronounced each word with exaggerated care. "What I mean is that Hebrew School is a pain even when the teachers are good. It's almost unbearable when they're bad. But I want to learn about being Jewish. The only place to learn in this town is at the Hebrew School. So, even if you would permit it, I'm not sure I'd quit."

"Admirably expressed, Abby," her father said, with a satisfied air.

"Why can't I feel the same way?" I asked.

"Well, you can," Abby said, "but you never did. Why would you, now that you've found out you're not Jewish?"

"Who says I'm not Jewish?" I exclaimed.

"The rabbi," Abby shot back.

"How does he know how I feel inside of me?" I returned, still angry.

"A Reform temple might bar mitzvah you," Mrs. Greenglass suggested. "According to many Reform rabbis, if you're brought up as a Jew, you're a Jew. They don't adhere to the tradition of the law in the same way a Conservative or Orthodox synagogue does."

"The nearest Reform temple is in Rivington," I said. "How would I get there? Anyway," I added uncomfortably, "to go there would be somehow—somehow evading the issue."

"Well, what is the issue?" Dr. Greenglass asked. Now he sounded less like a professor and more like a prosecutor.

"It isn't having or not having a bar mitzvah," I responded.

"Well, then," he persisted, "what is it?"

I shook my head.

"I think I know what it is," Abby interjected softly.

"Well, what is it?" Dr. Greenglass asked her.

"It's 'what is a Jew?' " Abby replied.

"For me," I said slowly, "it's what I think a Jew is. I have to decide. I have to decide for me."

Jewish law said I wasn't a Jew. My mother wasn't Jewish, so I wasn't Jewish.

But surely there was more to it than that. Surely how I felt inside my own self was what really mattered. Only I wasn't sure how I felt. I had to decide, deep down inside of me. Then I would decide what I wanted to do. I myself would decide what I wanted to do—not Pop, not my friends, not Abby, not even Rabbi Auerbach, but I myself.

CHAPTER EIGHT |

Two Saturdays later I went to the synagogue. I think it was the first time in my life I'd ever voluntarily entered the sanctuary. Every other time, I'd been dragged there by my father on a Jewish holiday, or else had gone on a Saturday morning because I'd been invited to a bar mitzvah and it was considered rude to attend the party Saturday afternoon, or Saturday night, or Sunday afternoon, and not go to the services first.

There was no bar or bat mitzvah that day. The congregation was small. I saw a few people I recognized, like old Mr. Surowitz, some of the other men from the minyan, and the entire Greenglass family. But Abby and Kenny weren't sitting with their parents. They were sitting over to the side with a whole bunch of other kids. To my surprise, I recognized seven or eight from my Hebrew School class, including both Howie and Morty. I hadn't known they came sometimes on a plain, ordinary Saturday morning, for no reason at all!

I didn't sit with them, though. I felt funny about it. I sat in the back. I don't think they even saw me. They actually ran a lot of the service. Howie led the congregation in singing one of the Psalms in Hebrew. Morty chanted the prayers accompanying the return of the Torah scroll to the ark, also in Hebrew, of course. I hadn't even known they could do those things, which was all the more reason to stay where I was. Next to them, I'd look like a fool.

But the rabbi knew I was there. Before the Torah is returned to the ark, the cantor carries it around the synagogue, followed by the rabbi and the president of the congregation. Everyone runs to the aisle to touch the Torah, the men with their prayer shawls, the women with their prayer books. The rabbi shakes hands, and both he and the cantor offer Sabbath greetings. "Shabbat shalom, Mrs. Levy. Gut Shabbes, Mr. Surowitz." And so on and so forth.

Even though I hadn't rushed to the aisles like the others, the rabbi found me as he walked past the very last row of pews. He held out his hand. Of course, I had to take it. "Shabbat shalom, Vic," he said. "It's nice to see you here."

"May I speak to you after services?" I asked.

He nodded. "Of course. After Kiddush."

Kenny Greenglass chanted the haftarah. It wasn't his bar mitzvah—he was already sixteen—but he chanted it anyway. The Greenglass family made the Kiddush in his honor. It wasn't fancy, like after a bar mitzvah—just some gefilte fish balls, challah, cake, and wine. I left the sanctuary before "Adon Olam," the final hymn, and peeked into the social hall, where I saw the table laid out. That's how I knew I wouldn't miss much by not going in. I didn't want to hang around. I didn't want to have to listen to a lot of comments from Howie or Morty. I didn't want to be subjected to the third degree from Mr. Greenglass or to sympathetic glances from Mrs. Greenglass. I didn't want to have to explain why I was there to anyone else, since I hadn't yet explained it to myself.

So I went into the rabbi's office and waited for him there. I didn't switch on the light, and the room had no window. The only illumination came through the glass door from the corridor. I sat silently in the black chair, waiting. After a long time, the door opened and the rabbi came in.

"Hello, Rabbi," I said quietly.

He jumped a foot off the ground. "Oh, Vic!" he exclaimed. "You startled me. I didn't see you."

"I've been waiting for you," I said.

He sat down next to me. "I thought you'd gone. I didn't see you at Kiddush and I thought you'd gone."

"I didn't want to talk to anyone," I said. "I didn't want anyone to ask me why I was in shul."

Through the dimness, I could see Rabbi Auerbach's eyes scrutinizing my face. "Why *are* you in shul?"

"I want to tell you something," I said. "I've thought about it and thought about it almost a week and want to tell you about it."

"I'm listening." The rabbi's voice was quiet; he sounded curious.

For a moment the silence lay between us. "I want to explain something to you," I said at last.

"Go ahead," he said.

"Don't interrupt."

"I won't."

"Promise? Even if what I say sounds silly? Not right, even, to say in a synagogue?"

"You mean sacrilegious?" he asked.

"Yes."

"There's nothing you can say," he replied softly, "that God hasn't heard, and forgiven. Go ahead."

"It isn't bad," I assured him.

"Well, I'm glad to hear that," he said. There was a ghost of a smile in his voice. "Sacrilegious and bad are not exactly the same thing, after all. So, go ahead."

I found it hard to speak. My ideas were not easy to say out loud. But at last I took the plunge. "You remember that guy who ran a diner out in Rivington? The one who had the sex change operation? It was all over the papers."

I thought I heard him gulp a little. But all he said was "Yes, I remember."

"I read this interview with him in the *Gazette.*" Beginning had been difficult, but, now that I'd started, the words came rushing out of my mouth. "He said he'd always felt that he really was a woman down inside. He'd felt that way from the time he was a tiny child. He said he'd always been a woman, trapped in a man's body. All the operation was going to do, he said, was make his body match his true inner self."

"His soul," the rabbi suggested.

"Yes," I said. "His soul. Well, down inside, it can be that way with a Jew. Just because a person isn't a Jew according to the rules doesn't change the way he feels inside. Just like that guy. He was a woman. And no matter what other people said, no matter what it looked like to them, he knew he was a woman."

"Well," the rabbi said, rubbing his chin, "I really don't think it's quite the same thing. . . ."

"Yeah, I know," I agreed. "Maybe that guy was crazy. A person who feels that he's Jewish isn't necessarily crazy."

"Not necessarily," the rabbi replied. There was an ironic edge to his voice. "What are you trying to tell me, Vic?" he went on. "What are you trying to say?"

I didn't reply.

"Are you saying that you're thinking about conversion?" the rabbi asked. "Are you thinking about it so you'll match, like the man from Rivington?"

"It's a consideration," I said slowly. "That's all. A consideration."

The rabbi nodded. Even in the dimness, I could see him nod. "If you ask me to convert you, I must answer no three times," he said. "You see, according to the Talmud, the rabbi must make sure the convert is totally sincere. We must make sure that he or she really *feels* Jewish, just as you suggest. We have to make sure he or she isn't doing it for someone else's sake. Do you understand?"

"Yes," I said. "Of course, I understand."

The rabbi stood up. "Well, Vic," he said, "I will count this as the first time."

I stood up, too. "There may never be a second time," I said.

"I know that," the rabbi said. "It is not my right to persuade you. But I'm always here to talk to you." He held out his hand. "Shabbat shalom, Vic," he said. "I look forward to hearing from you again soon."

"Shabbat shalom, Rabbi," I returned. And then I left.

CHAPTER NINE |

The day after I'd socked Stewie, I'd rushed down to the lunchroom and grabbed a seat at our usual table before I'd even bought anything to eat. I'd been the first person at the table, which was just what I'd intended. I wasn't going to give up eating with my friends just because Stewie and I had had a fight. He was going to have to avoid me, if he wanted to.

Which is what he did for a couple of weeks. He ate at a different table with Arnold and a couple of other creeps.

But the Monday after I'd been to the synagogue, things changed. I didn't rush, because I didn't think I had to any longer, and he did. By the time I got to the table, he was already seated there, and so was Arnold. I was mad, but I decided to sit down, anyway. Who was he to drive me away from Pat and Morty and Big John?

"Hi, Vic," Stewie said. He said it very loud, so I couldn't avoid hearing him.

"Hi, Stewie," I replied as I sat down. OK, I thought, if he's decided to be big about the whole thing, I wasn't going to be the one to act like a sorehead. After all, we'd been friends since fourth grade.

"I want to talk to you, Vic," he said.

"Oh, yeah?" I asked suspiciously. "What about?"

"Like, I'm sorry about the pennies."

I took a bite out of my hot dog. No one else said anything, either. They were all very quiet, listening to what was going to happen between Stewie and me.

"I didn't mean anything by it," he went on. "Nothing about Jews. I've got nothing against Jews. It was Abby I wanted to get at, that's all."

"She's only a girl," I said.

"But you have to admit, she's a pain in the ass," Stewie said. "I mean she'd be a pain in the ass if she were Italian or Irish or Chinese."

I still didn't think he'd have thrown pennies at her if she'd been Italian or Irish or Chinese. He'd have done something else. But he was trying, and I didn't want to see the gang split up because of him and me. "I'm sorry I hit you," I said slowly. "I just lost my temper, that's all. I didn't really know what I was doing."

"Shake," Big John said. "You two guys should shake."

So I put out my hand, and Stewie took it, and we shook, hard. After that Stewie acted as if nothing had happened. I tried to act that way, too, but I didn't find it so easy.

Maybe that explains what happened. I was being especially nice to Stewie, as if to make up for the doubts he didn't even know about, doubts that were living silently, deep in my heart. We had a day off from school Wednesday for teachers' in-service training, whatever that was. Stewie asked me to go downtown with him. Pat couldn't go; his mother worked and he had to baby-sit his younger brother and sister. Big John and Morty couldn't go, either. Morty's mother was taking him shopping for his bar mitzvah suit. Big John had just made the basketball team's starting lineup, and they were having an all-day practice. "Cripes," Stewie complained when he heard their excuses, "am I going to have to drag around the whole day myself? You'll come with me, won't you, Vic? There're some things I have to do."

"Sure, I'll come," I said.

But when I met him Wednesday morning at the bus station, he wasn't alone. Arnold was with him. What Stewie needed me for if he had that creep along, I didn't know, but it was too late to back out now.

We walked slowly up Main Street. It was a sunny, pleasant day for November, and it was good to be outdoors. But I wondered why we were downtown instead of at the shopping center. "What did we come here for?" I asked Stewie. "There's no place like Playland here. We can't play Galaxia or Space Invaders."

"They don't know us so well down here," Stewie said. "I'm afraid they're getting on to us at the shopping center. We've ripped those places off too often."

I was really annoyed. I hadn't known the whole purpose of the day was shoplifting. But it was my own fault. I should have asked. Now I was stuck.

But I wasn't worried, or afraid. I was afraid of a lot of things no one even knew about. Shoplifting wasn't one of them. After all, we'd been doing it on and off for a year or more, and nothing had ever happened to us. And nothing happened to us that day, either—at first. We went in and out of the five-and-ten and a couple of drug stores without any trouble. Then Stewie said he wanted to go into Lippman's Jewelers.

"What for?" I protested. "You think they're going to have gold necklaces lying around on the counters the way they did at Ekhart's?" The stores in the shopping center were mostly chains, owned by blocks of anonymous shareholders no one had ever seen or heard of. But Mr. Lippman lived in town. I'd never actually met him, but I'd seen him around. I knew who he was, even if he didn't know who I was. Grandma and Mrs. Lippman belonged to the same stock club.

"I just want to look," Stewie said.

"And even if they do have jewelry sitting out on counters," I added, "what can you do with it?"

"That's Arnold's job," Stewie said. "He knows where to get rid of things. He got me good money for the necklaces."

"From who?" I asked, curious.

Arnold shrugged. "I don't know," he said. "I give them to my cousin Hermie. He's in high school. He knows a lot of people."

"I got fifteen dollars for each necklace." Stewie

sounded pleased with himself, but I didn't think that was so wonderful. Each of those necklaces had sold for more than a hundred dollars, and that was with a discount.

"If you don't mind," I said, "I'll just skip Lippman's. If all you're going to do is case the joint, you don't need me."

"Yes, we do," Stewie said. He looked at me steadily. "Actually, we have a plan. I'm going to say I'm buying a gold watch for my father's birthday—"

"No one'll believe you," I interrupted. "Where would a kid like you get enough money for a gold watch?"

"I'll say the whole family is in on it—"

"And they sent you, the kid, to make the purchase?" I retorted sarcastically. "Don't be ridiculous."

"So if it doesn't work, it doesn't work," Stewie said. "We haven't lost a thing. But if the salesman does take the watches out, Arnold will distract him and you and I will swipe a couple if we can."

"The whole idea sounds crummy to me," I muttered.

"Oh, come on, old buddy," Stewie said cheerfully. "It's no different from what we've done a hundred times."

It was different, and I knew it. But I went into the store with Stewie and Arnold, anyway. Stewie was supposed to be my friend. I couldn't let him think he wasn't.

Lippman's was the fanciest jewelry store in New Hebron, but it wasn't busy on a Wednesday morning. There was only one clerk in the whole place when we walked in, and he was a jerk. He didn't even blink an eye when Stewie said he was looking for a gold wrist watch. He took a whole tray of them out of the case. Stewie and I leaned over them with great interest. Arnold wandered off, looking into the other cases. After a while, he called out, "Hey, mister, I got to get my girlfriend a charm bracelet. Can I look at these?"

"In a minute, young fellow," the sales clerk said.

"Oh, that's all right," Stewie interjected generously. "Go help him while I look these over. I have to decide between the one with the black face and the one with the calendar." He turned to me. "Which one do you like better?"

The sales clerk walked behind the counter toward Arnold. He leaned down to open the case holding the charm bracelets. Moving his hand so quickly I could scarcely see it, Stewie snatched one of the watches from the tray—not one of the two between which he was supposedly making his choice, but another one, a more expensive one, made in Switzerland. He dropped the watch into his pocket.

No sooner had the watch disappeared from view than a loud bell rang throughout the store. I was so startled by the sound that my whole body shivered at once. Stewie drew his breath in sharply. From the workroom in back of the store, Mr. Lippman himself hurried into view. The clerk stood up, a satisfied smirk on his face. "I caught them, Mr. Lippman," he shouted. "I caught them red-handed."

"Run for it," Stewie called. He dashed for the door.

"Don't bother," the clerk said. "I locked the door at

the same time I set off the alarm. We have two little buttons down there. Actually," he added, "we have three. A silent alarm, for people with guns."

"The police will be here in a minute," Mr. Lippman said. "You can turn off the alarm now, Mercer." The clerk leaned over, and the unbearable clanging stopped. I could only feel relieved at that.

"Do you really think we need the police?" I asked, keeping my voice as calm as I could. "Give it to him, Stewie. Give him the watch."

Stewie walked back to the counter. He took the watch out of his pocket and laid it back on the tray. "I'm sorry," he said in a low voice. "I didn't know what I was doing. Something just came over me when the clerk walked away. It was silly of him to leave the watches alone."

"I did it on purpose, you fool," the clerk said. Apparently it was we, not he, who were the jerks. "I knew why you kids were in here. Who ever heard of a family sending the kid to buy a gold watch?"

I managed not to say, "I told you so." We were in enough trouble already without quarreling among ourselves. I felt icy cold, but at the same time my palms were sweating. "Nothing really happened," I said. "Please don't turn us over to the police. Our parents will kill us."

Mr. Lippman laughed harshly. "You should have thought of that before you started in with me, young man," he said. "I certainly am going to turn you over to the police. Every shopkeeper on Main Street has trouble with you kids. Out at the shopping center, too. I'm glad Mercer caught you. It's about time someone made an example of you."

I bit my lips hard to keep the tears from forming. Everything, everything was about to tumble down around me, and I knew it as well as I knew my own name. Victor Abrams, tough guy. But this tough I wasn't. This tough I didn't want to be. Shoplifting was all right so long as we didn't get caught. I had never counted on getting mixed up with the police.

Two of them were banging at the door. Mr. Lippman let them in with his key. A few people had gathered on the sidewalk behind them. A woman and a man wearing a golf cap followed the cops through the door.

"I'm glad to see my new alarm system is working," Mr. Lippman said. "It rang in the police station all right, didn't it?"

The older cop nodded. "Yes, sir," he said. "The dispatcher radioed us." He tapped the walkie-talkie sticking out of his pocket. At least he hadn't entered the store with his gun drawn. He must have looked through the glass and seen it was only us. "What's the problem?" he asked, his eyes hastily surveying the entire place.

"Shoplifters," Mr. Lippman replied shortly. "These three boys."

"What did they take?" the cop asked.

"Nothing," Stewie said sullenly.

"I must warn you," the cop said. "Anything you say may be held against you."

"That one," Mr. Lippman said, jerking his head in

Stewie's direction, "that one took a watch. I got it back, thanks to Mercer's quickness. The other two are his confederates. They work as a team."

"A team, huh?" The cop's eyebrows shot up. "Do you wish to press charges?"

"You have the watch, Mr. Lippman," I begged. "Please don't press charges."

"I'm pressing charges," Mr. Lippman announced firmly. "I'm pressing charges against all three of them. Is that clear?"

The cop nodded.

"I want to make an example of these boys. I'm going to call the paper."

This time the cop shook his head. "They're juveniles, Mr. Lippman. The papers are not permitted to print their names."

"Honest people have no protection these days," Mr. Lippman snapped. "The only people the law protects are the criminals."

"Throw the book at them," the man in the golf cap grumbled.

The cop didn't answer either of them. "All right, boys," he said. "Let's go." He gave me a shove toward the door. I shivered under his touch, but I didn't say anything.

His sidekick grabbed Stewie and Arnold. "You don't have to push me," Stewie complained. "I'll go on my own steam."

Shut up, Stewie, I willed with all my mind. Shut up.

The assistant cop said it for me. "Shut up, boy." Stewie shut up. Mercer, Mr. Lippman, the man in the golf cap, and the woman stared at us silently as we marched out of the store. Stewie and Arnold kept their eyes focused on their feet, as if they were afraid a battery of TV cameras from the six o'clock news was waiting for them outside the door. I walked with my head up.

The cops ordered the three of us into the back seat of the cop car parked at the curb. A grill separated us from the front seat, where the policemen sat. I felt as if I were in jail already.

When we got to the station, they wrote down our names, addresses, and phone numbers. They told us to empty our pockets. They found the stuff we'd taken from the drugstores and the five-and-ten—tubes of Chap Stick, AAA batteries, ball point pens, a Louis L'Amour paperback western. That was too bad. It made it impossible for us to pretend that the watch was the first thing we'd ever tried to lift in all our pure, innocent lives.

Stewie complained the whole time. Arnold and I kept our mouths shut. I was feeling too sick to say anything, even if I wanted to. I tried not to think about what was coming next.

But it came. The cop behind the desk called our parents. He had to. They weren't allowed to question us unless one of our parents was present. When I told him my folks were divorced, he asked me which one I lived with, and that's who he called. I knew Pop would be apoplectic at being interrupted at work, just for starters. Where he'd go from there, I couldn't even imagine. He'd been called in to see teachers, to see a principal, to see the rabbi—but not the cops, not before this.

"Cripes," Stewie exclaimed in a loud voice, "I'm in for it now. My old man'll beat me to a pulp. It'll be your fault," he told the cop behind the desk. "I'll sue."

The cop stared at Stewie for a long moment. Then he said, "Mr. Brisbane, you don't seem to understand. You are suspected of committing a crime." He emphasized the word "suspected" in an ironic way. "A real honest-to-goodness crime. If I were your father, I'd break both your legs, and that would just be the beginning."

Stewie quieted down for a while. We sat in a row on a bench, like the three monkeys on my mother's knick-knack shelf. Their names were See No Evil, Hear No Evil, and Speak No Evil. She didn't take much when she moved out, but she took them.

Stewie's and Arnold's mothers came a few minutes later. They worked close by. First Arnold, and then Stewie, with their mothers, went with the police lieutenant into another room. What with the police radio, the telephone, and the constant traffic in and out of the station, I couldn't have heard what was going on in there if I'd been sitting right next to the door, and I wasn't. When Arnold and his mother came out, they walked right past me without saying a word. Stewie kind of waved at me. His mother gave me a dirty look, as if, somehow, it was all my fault.

It took Pop a long time to get in from the city. He couldn't ask Mom to come instead. She was out of town. I just had to sit on that bench and wait for him. I had plenty of time to think about how I'd messed it all up.

Just as I'd been beginning to straighten it all out in my head, I'd messed it all up. All the kids thought I was so smart, so cool. Now they'd find out the truth. I was dumb, and I was scared.

Pop was smoldering when he walked into the police station. He'd had a whole hour on the train to work up a real good head of anger, plus ten minutes more as he drove from the train station to the police station. "I don't care if you throw the book at him," he said to the cop behind the desk. "He deserves it." Those were the first words out of his mouth.

The lieutenant said, "We'll talk about it in here, Mr. Abrams." We went into the other room, the one in which Arnold and Stewie had been questioned. I was surprised. It was like a regular office. I guess maybe I had expected medieval torture machines.

"Sit down," the lieutenant said. He spoke quite pleasantly as he gestured to two chairs near the desk. He took the one behind the desk and immediately pressed a button on a machine. "I want you to know," he said, "that I'm taping our entire conversation." He looked at me, then he looked at Pop, then he looked back at me again. "You know," he said, "Arnold and Stewart admitted they were shoplifting today. As a matter of fact, this isn't the first time we've picked Arnold up. The Juvenile Aid Bureau has dealt with him before."

That was interesting. I hadn't known that. Apparently, everyone didn't have to find out. That made me feel a little better. But only for a moment. I couldn't depend on Stewie to keep his trap shut. Or Mr. Lippman, once the cops told him who we were.

And of course Pop knew. That was the main thing. Pop knew.

The lieutenant opened a little paper bag that was sitting on his desk and poured its contents onto the blotter. "Well, Victor," he said, "do you recognize these things?" His tone was quiet, matter-of-fact.

I looked at the Chap Sticks, the pens, the packages of M & M's, and all the other stuff that tumbled out on top of his desk. "Yes," I muttered.

"Speak up, Victor," the lieutenant said. "I can't hear you."

"Yes," I repeated, only a little louder. But I guess the lieutenant heard me that time, because Pop certainly did. His hands were clenching the arms of his chair so tightly his knuckles had turned white. I think he was doing that to keep himself from jumping up and punching me in the jaw.

"Where did these things come from?" the lieutenant asked.

"Out of my pockets," I replied.

"Had you used them?"

I shook my head.

"You can't just gesture, Victor," the policeman reminded me sharply. "You have to speak, and you have to speak up."

I sighed. "No," I said.

"Where was the stuff before it was in your pockets?"

"White's Drug Store," I said. "Rexall Drugs. The Broadway Five-and-Ten. Meinert's Hardware."

"Did you steal it from those places, Victor?" He

didn't sound angry. He didn't sound anything. His voice was flat and cold.

"Yes," I said.

"What about Lippman's?" he asked me. "Did you take anything from Lippman's?"

I shook my head.

"I told you before," he reminded me, annoyed now. "You must speak, and you must speak up."

"No. I didn't take anything from Lippman's."

"But you went into that store."

"Yes."

"Who with?"

"With Arnold and Stewie." Why was he asking questions to which he already knew the answers?

"Why?"

"Stewie asked me to."

"Why?"

I didn't answer.

"Tell him why," Pop barked. "And tell him the truth."

"Cover," I said. "Arnold and I were supposed to cover for Stewie."

Then he asked me a lot more questions. He made me tell him exactly what had happened inside Lippman's. He didn't let me leave out a thing.

Finally he asked me one more question. "Have you ever been involved in shoplifting before?" His eyes rested on my face.

I could have lied. He could prove what had happened that day, but it would be nearly impossible for him to prove what had happened in the past. Only I didn't lie. I don't know why, but I didn't. I'd never been in the habit of lying, I guess. It was sort of a matter of pride. So I didn't really know how to begin. "Yes," I said. "But I won't do it again." I returned his glance as I spoke.

The lieutenant's eyes held mine for a moment, but he made no comment. Then he spoke to my father. "That'll be all for today," he said. "You can take him home. You'll have to come into the Juvenile Aid Bureau to sign the transcript of our conversation. You'll receive a summons in the mail telling you when to appear in Juvenile Court for a hearing. The Bureau's intake social worker will be in touch with you prior to that date, for an interview. Do you understand, Mr. Abrams?"

"Yes, Lieutenant," my father replied.

"And you, Victor? Do you understand?"

"Yes, I understand," I replied.

The lieutenant stood up. So did Pop and I. We walked out of the office together. "We'll be keeping an eye on you, Victor," the lieutenant said. "Don't try anything in the meantime."

He didn't have to say that. Hadn't I told him I wouldn't do it again?

"Thank you, Lieutenant," Pop said.

Thank you? Thank you for what?

Pop and I walked to the car without a word passing between us. But once we were in it, he had plenty to say. He said more in ten minutes than he had in two years. "This is the last straw," he began. "Absolutely the last straw." He didn't shut up all the way home. "Haven't I given you everything you ever needed?

Everything you ever wanted? And what have I gotten from you in return? Nothing but trouble. What's your grandmother going to say? What're your uncles going to say? My son the shoplifter. My son the thief. O my God!" He said the same things over and over again. I wanted to put my hands up over my ears to block out the sound of his voice. But I didn't, because it wouldn't have done any good. I would have gone on hearing his words in my head. "My son the shoplifter. My son the thief. O my God!"

When we got home my father told me I was not to leave the house except to go to school until further notice. He also withdrew my allowance. I didn't care. There was nowhere I wanted to go and no one I wanted to see, anyhow. I didn't even want to go to school the next day. Would the other kids have found out by then? If they did know, what would I say to them? I could brazen it out, somehow, I supposed. But I didn't want to. That would take energy. I didn't seem to have any left.

Pop went out to have supper with Mrs. Kirsch. What was to stop me from leaving the house once he was gone? He couldn't even stay home with me one night to make sure I obeyed him. But I did obey him. Like I said, there was nowhere I wanted to go and no one I wanted to see.

I lay on my bed staring at the ceiling. The TV was on, but I didn't look at it. It was just a buzzing in the background. I don't know how long I lay there, not really awake, not really asleep. After a while the phone rang. I picked it up without thinking. If I'd thought about it,

I'd have just let it ring, because I certainly didn't want to talk to anyone, particularly not to anyone who'd be calling me, like one of the guys. But answering a phone is an automatic reflex. The message to pick up the receiver goes right from your ear to your arm, without giving your brain a chance to say no.

"Hello," I mumbled.

"Hello," the voice on the other end replied. "Vic?"

"Yeah. Who's this?" I didn't recognize the voice. It certainly wasn't one of the guys'.

"Rabbi Auerbach. How're you doing?"

"Rabbi Auerbach?" Had he found out already? Was he calling to tell me how glad he was I wasn't a Jew after all?

"Yes. I just phoned to see how you are." I recognized his voice now, dry and ironic. The only reason I hadn't known whose it was from the beginning was the unexpectedness of hearing it.

"I'm fine," I said. I certainly was in perfect health.

"When you left Saturday," he said, "I thought you looked a bit troubled. I thought maybe you'd call, or come around again."

"I'm OK," I said. "Thanks for asking."

"Well, that's my job," he said pleasantly.

"Even if I'm not a member of your congregation?" I said.

"You've made up your mind about that?" It was half a statement, half a question.

"Was there ever any doubt?" I returned.

"Well, yes," the rabbi said quietly. "I rather thought there was—a doubt, that is."

"Well, there isn't," I said.

"You don't have to make a definite statement right this minute," the rabbi said. "I'd like you to come in and talk about it with me some more."

"No, I don't want to do that," I said. He would never convert me now, even if I asked him twenty times. Who would want a preteen hood in his religion, if he hadn't been stuck with him from the beginning?

"No?" He sounded a little surprised. "Well, then, I'll just keep in touch."

I hesitated. I wanted to say, "Don't bother," but I didn't want to be rude to him. He'd been nice enough to call, nice enough to care. I was still debating how to respond when he ended the conversation. "Good-bye, Vic. Give me a ring any time, if you want to."

"Good-bye, Rabbi," I replied. I waited until I'd heard the click of his receiver as he hung it up, and then I put mine back, too.

CHAPTER TEN |

My alarm rang at six A.M. I'd set it so early because I wanted to be sure to catch Pop before he left the house. I wanted to talk to him.

I threw an old bathrobe on over my underwear and pattered downstairs barefoot, shivering in the early-morning chill. Pop was standing at the kitchen counter, drinking instant coffee and looking at the front page of the newspaper. He glanced up when I walked in the room and kind of grunted.

"Pop," I said, "I don't feel so hot."

"I'm not surprised," he said. "Criminals who've been caught don't usually feel too good."

"So I lifted a couple of tubes of Chap Stick and some batteries," I responded sharply, my voice loud and angry. "You talk as if I were a murderer."

"I don't like living with a criminal," Pop retorted. "I think you had better live with your mother for a while. I, for one, have had it with you. Let's see how she manages."

"Are you going to tell her?" I asked. I was pleading now. "Please don't tell her."

"Of course I'm going to tell her," he snapped. "She's your parent too, just as much as I am. She has to know. Why should I be the one to have all the trouble all the time?"

"She'll never take me," I said. "Not full time. Especially not if you tell her."

"Well," he said, "we'll see about that." He folded up his newspaper and stuck it in his briefcase. "Anyway," he added, "how do you plan to hide it from her?"

"The paper doesn't print the names of juvenile offenders," I said.

"You think Mr. Lippman is going to keep your precious secret? He's got the biggest mouth in New Hebron. It'll be all over town by three o'clock this afternoon—if it isn't already."

"I've got this stomach ache, Pop," I said. "I'm not going to school today."

"Cut the crap," Pop shot back. "You'll go to school. You have to face the music sooner or later. It might as well be sooner. I don't want you hanging around the house all day. Who knows what mischief you'll get into?" He'd left his coat hanging on the back of a kitchen chair the night before. He reached for it now and put it on. "I'll call your guidance counselor later this morning," he said. "I'll make sure you're in school." Without another word he picked up his briefcase and walked out of the room. He didn't say good-bye.

The only reason I'd gotten up to tell him I didn't want to go to school was that it was Mrs. Harter's day to come to clean. She always left Pop a note telling him just what she'd done, as if he cared. If I happened to be home, she fussed over me as if I were her lost chick. That's because she got bored in the house alone all day and liked someone to talk to. But in her note she'd let Pop know how well she'd taken care of me. So I couldn't stay home that day without his finding out.

I could have hung around downtown or at the shopping center till three o'clock. But that wouldn't have been much better than going to school. I was bound to run into someone I knew sooner or later. Maybe that person would already know about what had happened yesterday, and maybe he'd ask me about it. New Hebron was a lot bigger than it had been when Pop was growing up, but it was still a small town.

So I knew I might just as well go to school. That really wasn't such a bad thing. If I stayed out more than two days, the attendance officer would call. As Pop had said, I had to face the music sooner or later. So let it be sooner.

Morty and Howie were standing by the lockers, talking to Stewie. In spite of the crowds in the hall, I could see them all the way from the other end. Stewie was waving his hands around excitedly and talking in a loud voice. The last person I wanted to see that morning was

Stewie. But my locker was there. I had to hang up my jacket. I had to get my books. I walked toward them slowly.

Stewie saw me coming. "Hi, old buddy," he shouted. "How are you this morning? All recovered from the third degree?" He had a grin on his face as broad as a crocodile's.

"What third degree?" I opened my locker and hung my jacket on the hook inside.

"Didn't the cops beat you up, too?" Howie asked. "The way they beat up Stewie?" His eyes were wide with wonder and admiration. He thought Stewie and I were heroes. The jerk.

I looked at Stewie. He shrugged very slightly. I felt like throwing up right then and there. I took my books off the locker shelf and slammed the door shut. "I'll see you guys later," I said. I walked to homeroom by myself.

It was all over school, just as I had feared. Only it wasn't Mr. Lippman who was the source of all the talk. It was Stewie himself. From the way he'd told the story, and from the way some of the other kids looked at us, you'd have thought he and I were Robin Hood, or Zorro, or someone like that.

In social studies we were making relief maps out of flour-and-water paste. We were working in groups. Debbie Barton and I were in the same one. "Hey," she said as we leaned over our large piece of cardboard spread out on the floor, "you OK?"

"Of course I'm OK," I said.

"The cops didn't hurt you?"

"I'm fine," I replied almost angrily. "The cops didn't hurt me, and they didn't hurt Stewie."

"You guys really stood up to those pigs." I don't think she'd even heard what I had said. "That's what Stewie told me. You guys really got guts."

I pretended I was too busy making the Rocky Mountains to answer her.

She was not deterred. "Too bad you got caught. But now you're wise. You won't get caught again." She touched my arm. I had to look at her. She smiled. "You know those little ivory earrings that look like tiny flowers? I like them."

"Tell Stewie," I said very slowly and very clearly. "He's your boyfriend."

She pouted, like a five-year-old. "No, he isn't," she said. "Why does everyone think that? Just because he likes me doesn't mean I have to like him. I can like other people," she added significantly.

"We need more paste," I said. I got up and walked to the table at the back of the room where the supplies were laid out for us. There were just a few minutes left in the period, and I managed not to return.

Later I walked to lunch with Morty. "Listen," I said, "the cops didn't beat us up. They didn't touch us. That's a whole bunch of baloney. And we didn't get away with anything. Stewie had to give the watch back. Thank goodness. If he hadn't, things would go a lot worse for us when we show up in court, and they're going to be bad enough as it is."

"Yeah," Morty said, "I know. Stewie exaggerates. No one pays any attention to him."

"But they do," I said. "He has them convinced we didn't do anything wrong."

"Well, you didn't," Morty said. "Anyway, nothing *really* wrong. You didn't do anything a lot of the rest of us don't do all the time. You just got caught, that's all."

"I'm not doing it anymore," I said.

Morty nodded. "Of course not. It's too risky for you now."

"I don't think you ought to do it, either," I suggested. "The cops didn't beat us up, but, believe me, it was no fun to be picked up. I was no hero. I was scared out of my pants. And my father's ready to throw me out of the house. I mean, who needs it?"

"You can come stay with me if your mother won't have you," Morty said.

"You think so?" I asked. "If my own folks don't want me, what makes you think your folks will?"

"Well," Morty said, "I'll ask them."

At lunch, Big John made the same offer. But I knew that his parents liked me even less than Morty's. All my friends were dreaming. And the funny thing was that I was the only person who knew it.

Well, maybe not quite the only person. The first time I passed Abby in the hall, she didn't say hello to me. So the next time I saw her, I said hello to her. She looked at me as if I were an empty space. There wasn't even a flicker of recognition in her eye. And that happened two more times in the course of the day.

And so, after school, I got on my bike and pedaled

over to her house. She walked home, so I got there a good while before I could expect her. I sat on her front steps and waited. I waited for a long time, maybe an hour, much longer than it would have taken her if she had come right home after school. By the time I saw her turn the corner and come strolling down the street, I was really mad at her. I knew that was ridiculous, but I had been annoyed with her to start with.

When she saw me sitting on the steps, she stopped still in her tracks. When she started walking again, she hurried. "What are you doing here?" she asked as soon as she got close enough for me to hear her. She actually sounded angry.

"What took you so long?" I retorted.

She frowned. "What business is that of yours?" She was standing still again, at the end of the walk. What did she think I was going to do, grab her when she passed me? I'd as soon have grabbed a porcupine.

"I've been waiting an hour for you," I said.

"How was I supposed to know?" She took two steps forward. "I stayed for a Drama Club meeting." She stared at me, still frowning. "If you're looking for my mother, she's at her office."

"What would I want with your mother?"

"You need a lawyer, don't you?" She bit off each word sharply in that way she had when she was cross.

"What do you think I am?" I cried. "Some kind of criminal? Is that why you won't talk to me?"

Abby nodded. "You got it," she said quietly.

I rose from the steps and walked toward her. "You *are* a priss," I said. "I always knew it. No one's mad at me, except my father and you. What gives you the right to judge me?"

"I liked you," she said, as if that explained something.

Like can have a lot of different meanings. "You mean like like, the way Stewie likes Debbie Barton?" I asked.

"Yes," she said. "I never told anyone. They would have just laughed. You would have just laughed, if you'd found out. But I don't like you anymore. You're a thief."

I shook my head in amazement. "Why?" I asked slowly. "Why did you like me?"

"I didn't know you were a thief," Abby said with an exasperated expression. "I mean I knew you were kind of wild, but I never thought you'd done anything really wrong. You're very smart, and you must know what you look like."

"No, I don't," I snapped.

She walked past me now. "Don't talk dumb," she said. "You do, too, just as I know what I look like. You want me to say it?" She had reached the steps, and she turned around to face me. "Do you want me to say it right out loud? Everyone knows you're the best-looking guy at New Hebron Middle School. The best-looking guy in the seventh grade, anyway," she amended. "And the most popular, I guess. That's who you are—you're the king of the seventh grade."

I squirmed inside my jacket, I felt so hot and uncomfortable. "Cut the crap," I muttered.

"The king of the seventh grade," she repeated, as if she hadn't even heard me. "After all," she added, her voice suddenly quiet, "a cat can look at a king."

I walked back up the path and sat down on the bottom step. She sat down on the next one up. She had calmed down quite a bit. "I mean, I knew you'd never go out with me or anything like that," she said. "But I didn't really care about that. I just liked you. But I don't anymore. I can't like a thief. And I'm mad at you, too."

"Everybody does it," I defended myself. "I just got caught."

"Everybody doesn't do it," she retorted. "I don't."

"Oh, I mean every *regular* person," I tried to explain.

"So what am I? *Ir*regular?"

"I'm through with it," I told her. "I'm not going to do it anymore. It's too dangerous."

"Big deal," she scoffed. "So you're afraid now. But do you think what you did is wrong?"

"All I ever took were little things. Tapes and batteries and pens and things like that." I didn't mention stuffed mice.

"So what?" she asked. "If it belongs to someone else and you take it, you're stealing. It doesn't matter how big or little it is. It's stealing."

"Woolworth's isn't someone," I said. "Ekhart's isn't someone."

"Yes, they are," she said firmly. "If you don't know that, you don't know anything." She stood up again. "I have to go in now."

I stood up, too. "You're a priss, Abby Greenglass," I said. "You're a regular priss. Maybe someday you'll do something wrong. You're not perfect, you know. No one is."

She was already at the front door. "I never said I was," she shot back. Then she opened the door. She walked through, turned, and called to me, "Good-bye, Mr. Shoplifter," and slammed the door shut.

I liked her mother a lot. I liked her whole family a lot. Actually, I kind of envied them. But I didn't like her, and I wasn't going to have anything more to do with her. From now on, when I passed her in the hall at school, she could shout, "Hi, Vic!" in a voice as loud as a trumpet and I wouldn't answer her.

"Mr. Shoplifter." That's all I was to her, "Mr. Shoplifter." That was my identity. That's all I was to the whole bunch of them. To my father. To Stewie, and Morty, and Big John, and Howie. My father and Abby thought that made me a criminal. Stewie and Howie thought it made me a hero. It didn't change how Big John and Morty felt about me one way or the other. But to them all that's what I was. Mr. Shoplifter. Like Phil Lambert, the pothead, or Gloria Morris, who put out, now I was Vic Abrams, the shoplifter.

King of the seventh grade. King of the seventh grade? Some king.

CHAPTER ELEVEN |

"He's your son, too!" Pop screamed into the phone. "It's about time you started taking a little responsibility for him."

He was talking to my mother. He was in the kitchen and I was in the family room, but I could hear every word.

"What do you mean, you're away too much?" he repeated. "So stay home for a while. Would that be so terrible?"

I picked myself up and walked into the kitchen. Maybe I'm one of those sickies who enjoys torturing himself. Whatever the reason, I felt that I wanted to see Pop's face as well as hear what he was saying. After all, it was my fate he was discussing. He was just as angry as he'd been the day before. Mom had gotten home that very day, and he was making sure she knew all about everything.

His face was pale, and dark circles rimmed his eyes. As he spoke to my mother, he kept running his hand through his hair so that pieces of it were now standing up all over his head. He looked like a scarecrow. He didn't sound like one, though. He was roaring like a not-so-cowardly lion. I'd never heard him scream like that. "So what makes you think I want a criminal living with me? . . . Oh, so now it's my fault." Suddenly he wasn't yelling anymore, but his voice was heavy with irony. "Well, that's certainly a novel interpretation of the situation. . . ."

His eyes, dull and cold, were resting on me as he spoke. "He's right here," he said. "Talk to him yourself." He held the receiver out to me. I took it. He let go of it quickly, as if he feared some disease like leprosy might pass from me to him by way of the yellow plastic.

"Yeah, Mom," I said, keeping my voice as neutral as I could. I had no idea what was coming.

"I'm very disappointed in you, Vic," she said.

She was disappointed in me. That was interesting. I had never mentioned how disappointed I was in her. However, that moment didn't seem the time to bring it up.

"It was just a sort of game, Mom," I said. "I won't do it again. I promise."

"How can I believe that?" she asked.

I had no answer to that question, so I kept quiet.

"Well, you're in a mess, however you slice it," she

went on. "Your father says he wants you out of the house. I don't know where you're going to go. You certainly can't come here. We're away too much, and obviously you can't be trusted alone. Maybe there's some kind of home for boys like you." She wasn't angry. She wasn't screaming and yelling. Her voice was perfectly calm, as if she were talking about making an appointment for me with the dentist. "Maybe we can find one, and you can stay there until your father gets over being so mad."

"I could run away," I said.

"Don't you threaten me, Vic," she snapped.

"I didn't mean it as a threat, Mom," I said gloomily. "If I ran away, you'd both be rid of me. Your problem would be solved."

Pop had been standing by the kitchen door, listening. Now he just shook his head and walked out of the room.

"It's not my problem," Mom said. "It's your problem. Stop talking nonsense."

"This conversation wasn't my idea," I muttered.

"Well, then, perhaps we'd better end it," she replied shortly. "Good-bye, Vic." I heard the click of the receiver being replaced in its cradle before I even had a chance to reply. That was just as well. I certainly had nothing more that I wanted to say to her.

I walked into the family room. Pop had snapped on the TV. I sat down as far away from him as I could get. I couldn't even see the TV screen. He just kept staring at it, never even glancing in my direction.

Finally I couldn't stand the way he was acting any-more—as if I weren't in the room. It was I who had to speak. "I'm sorry, Pop," I said. I sort of yelled to make sure he heard me above the noise of the idiot box. "I won't do it again. I promise."

Still he did not take his eyes off the ancient episode of *The Honeymooners* he was watching. Actually, I've seen some of those shows. They're really pretty funny. But Pop wasn't cracking a smile. He was just staring. And he didn't say one word. But I knew he had heard me. I had spoken loud enough.

He was giving me the silent treatment. He did that a lot. I got that way sometimes myself, but I never went to his extreme. When he was really mad, he just pulled himself into a shell, like a turtle, and refused to speak to anyone at all. When he had acted like that, my mother had literally gone crazy. Once or twice she'd actually thrown things at him. It was one of the main reasons she had left him, I was sure. Yelling she could handle, but not a stone wall.

Well, I wasn't going to stand for it. I had done a wrong thing, a bad thing, but I was still his son. I didn't deserve the kind of treatment he was handing out. It's not right to ignore other people. It isn't much better than stealing.

I went upstairs. I took my knapsack down from the closet shelf. Inside it I put a flashlight, extra batteries, a couple of books, a transistor radio, a clean T-shirt, clean jockey shorts, my toothbrush, some toothpaste, a towel, a cake of soap, and the good penknife my grandfather had given me years before. My sleeping bag was up on the closet shelf, too. I hadn't used it since my short-lived Cub Scout days. I lifted it down. I put on my warm jacket. I stuck all the money I had into my wallet, and placed the wallet in my pocket.

Carrying the knapsack and the sleeping bag, I walked downstairs as quietly as I could. But it wouldn't have mattered if Pop had heard me on the steps or in the kitchen. He wouldn't have paid any attention.

I opened the refrigerator and removed a package of cheese, a loaf of bread, two cans of beer, two cans of 7-Up, and three apples. I stashed all the food in the knapsack, and then I slung it over my shoulders.

Leaving the house was trickier. Now I had to really make sure Pop didn't hear me, because he'd have noticed the back door closing. He'd forbidden me to leave the house, except to go to school, and he'd have come after me if he'd thought I was disobeying him.

Fortunately, the volume on the TV was turned up even louder than before. Maybe that was Pop's way of telling me not to even try to talk to him again. I tiptoed across the kitchen and into the back hall. Then I very, very slowly turned the back-door knob so that it wouldn't click. I opened the door carefully. If you opened it quickly, it squeaked. I slipped through it, and then I closed it just as slowly and carefully as I'd opened it. Once it was shut, I wanted to run. I resisted that impulse. If I hurried, I might bump into something, or fall, or otherwise make some kind of noise.

I'd counted on Pop's having left the garage door open. He usually did, and that night was no exception. I fastened my sleeping bag to my bike's back fender, and then I rolled the bike out of the garage and down to the end of the driveway.

I mounted up and pedaled down the street. "Good-bye, Pop," I whispered to myself. "Good-bye. If you don't want me around you, well, I don't want you around me, either." I wished I'd been able to say that to him before I'd left. But then, if I had, he'd have stopped me from going.

I headed for my grandmother's house. Not that I had any intention of letting her know I was there. I certainly didn't want to live with Mom and Bart, even if they'd been willing to have me. I mean, Pop and I had never exactly been buddies, but at least he was home now and then. I'd have rattled around in Mom's house like a solitary ghost. But even less than I wanted to stay with Mom and Bart did I want to stay with my grand-mother. Not that anyone had suggested such a thing—yet. Living with her would have been like living with your own private cop and judge rolled up into one person.

My grandmother's house was on maybe two acres of ground. My grandfather's workshop was at the opposite end of the lot from the house, behind the garage. A little lane ran alongside the property, so I was able to approach the workshop without even going up the driveway, which opened off the main road. I found a space in the hedges where some branches had died away, and I pushed my way through them.

Because of the position of the garage, the workshop wasn't visible from the house. I snapped on my flash-light, unlocked the padlock, walked inside, and shut the door behind me. I wished I could have padlocked the door again, but there was no way of doing that from the inside. And even though the shop wasn't visible from the house, I didn't want to risk turning on the lights. The flashlight would have to do.

The room was bitter cold, and the dust made me sneeze. I plugged in the electric heater. Then I cleared away a space on the floor next to it and spread out my sleeping bag. I opened my knapsack and laid everything that was in it out neatly on the work table. Grandpa had always kept the workshop in perfect order. I didn't want to change that.

By the time I'd arranged my stuff, the heater was beginning to take the chill out of the air. I made myself a sandwich out of bread and cheese. I opened a can of beer. I turned on the radio, keeping the volume very low. I took my book—*The Book of Lists*—and my sandwich and my beer and climbed into my sleeping bag.

Really, I was very comfortable. I tried not to think about what would happen tomorrow. Instead, I ate the sandwich and swallowed the can of beer. I wasn't used to drinking beer. Combined with the increasing heat in the room, it made me very sleepy. With the noise of the radio playing softly in my ears, my eyes shut before I'd finished even a page of the book. I fell fast asleep.

I don't know how long I slept. I awoke bathed in sweat. The room was too warm now, and pitch black. My flashlight had died. It wasn't the radio that had awakened me. It was still playing quietly. Maybe it was the heat, or my nightmare. I had been dreaming that I was at a fancy party. Maybe it was my own bar mitzvah reception—I'm not sure. All my relatives were there, though—my mother and Bart, my father and Mrs. Kirsch, my grandmother, my fat, shiny uncles with their wives glittering in gold necklaces, jangly bracelets, and diamond rings, and my snotty cousins in three-piece suits. They stood in a circle around me. One at a time, I waved at each of them with my hand. "You're dead," I said to each one in turn. The one I was speaking to didn't fall down, but I knew from the way his or her eyes and mouth stared at me that he or she was really dead. And the scariest part of all, the part that really made the dream a nightmare, was that I didn't care. I didn't feel anything at all.

I sat up in my sleeping bag and looked around. I couldn't see a single thing. It must have clouded over, because no light came in through the single dusty windowpane or under the door. I don't like the night much even when I'm in my own bed, and the shade is up, and moonlight fills my own familiar room. So it wasn't surprising that the small drop of panic that had never left me since the moment I'd heard the burglar alarm go off in Lippman's Jewelry Store now began to grow and grow until it filled my whole chest. I was scared to death. I was paralyzed with fear. I wanted to get up and feel on the table for the extra batteries so I could try to put them in my flashlight, even in the dark, and then see again. But I couldn't get up. I couldn't move.

Then I heard the noise. It was the crackle of footsteps on dead leaves and fallen twigs. It was close, right by the workshop. But I heard no voices. Someone, or more than one, was creeping up to my hideout. I didn't know who; I didn't know why. If the intruders were carrying a light, I couldn't see it; the window was on the side of the room opposite where the sound was coming from. My teeth began to chatter and, in spite of the heat, my palms were wet and cold.

The door creaked open. The beam of a lantern-sized flashlight shone in my face. I heard a long, sharp scream. Where did it come from? Out of my own mouth, I suddenly realized. Yet as the sound reached my ears I hadn't even known that it was I who was screaming.

"It's all right, Vic," a voice said. "Everything's all right." It was my father. His tone was low and reassuring. There was no anger in it. He entered the workshop. Someone else followed him. He set his light down on the table, and then I could see. The person who had followed him into the room was Rabbi Auerbach.

I found my voice. "Hi, Pop," I said. "Hi, Rabbi. I'm sorry I screamed. You guys scared me."

"You scared me," Pop said.

"Me too," Rabbi Auerbach agreed. They sat down, side by side, on the bench next to the table.

"You? I scared you? How could I do that?"

"For a smart boy, you can be pretty dumb," Rabbi Auerbach said. "Your father didn't know where you were. Of course he was scared."

"Oh." My fear had evaporated instantly. It was only a memory. Now I itched with curiosity. I wanted to know everything. "What are you doing here?" I asked him.

"I came to your house to see you," he replied. "It was

about ten o'clock, after my meeting. Your dad shouted for you to come down. You didn't answer, so he went upstairs to get you. When he came back, I could see how scared he was. White as a sheet. He said you were gone, and he said he had no idea where."

"I almost had a heart attack," Pop said. "Really, Vic, what's the big idea?" But still he didn't sound very angry. What he sounded was relieved. "Thank God, Rabbi Auerbach kept his head. I was all for going right to the police, but he suggested we try calling Morty and Big John first."

"I wasn't there," I said.

"You don't say," Rabbi Auerbach murmured.

"Then we called some of your other friends," Pop continued. "Then we called your mother. Of course, there was no answer at her house. So then Rabbi Auerbach asked me why you'd run away." He stopped talking. There was a slight frown on his face, and the dark circles around his eyes seemed deeper and blacker than the ones I'd seen there earlier in the evening. Our glances locked in a long look.

The question the rabbi had asked Pop was one I had to answer. "You didn't want me with you," I said. "Neither did Mom. But I don't want to live with her, either. Don't make me go there. Please don't."

"You don't want to live with her?" Pop actually sounded surprised.

"Did I ever say I did?" I asked.

"You're always telling me what a great guy Bart is," Pop replied slowly. "You're always talking about the great food your mother has around for you to eat."

I rubbed it into Pop sometimes. I knew that. "I don't want to live there," I repeated. "It would be too lonesome."

"You sure scared me," Pop said. "You scared the heart right out of me, running away like that. All I could see in my head was you getting off the bus at the terminal in the city, and some hustler coming up to you and offering you money and you ending up dead someplace."

"You see too many movies, Pop," I said. "I wouldn't go there. I'm not that dumb. But I had to go somewhere."

"You took me too seriously, Vic," Pop said. "I'd never have thrown you out of the house. Not really."

"Well, Pop," I said softly, "how was I supposed to know that?"

"You've both said and done things you're sorry for," Rabbi Auerbach interjected. He stood up. He was always standing up when he thought a conversation had gone on long enough. "I, for one, am tired. I want to go home and go to bed. I suggest that you two do the same."

I stood up, too, and began collecting my things. "Leave your bike here," Pop said. "We'll come back for it tomorrow. Grandma probably won't even notice it. She never comes back here. If she does say something, we'll think of an excuse."

"How did you know I was here?" That was another thing I was curious about.

"Rabbi Auerbach helped me figure that out." Pop picked up the beer cans and shoved them into my knapsack without saying a word about them. "After we realized you weren't at a friend's," he went on, "and you weren't at your mother's, the rabbi asked me if there was some place you loved, some sort of secret place where you felt good. I remembered the workshop. I remembered that whenever we have dinner with your grandmother, you come back here."

So he'd noticed. I hadn't known that. "I check things out," I explained to the rabbi. "I make sure they're just the way Grandpa left them."

"I didn't really think you'd be here, though," Pop said. "It seemed too obvious. If you were here it would seem that you weren't really . . ." His voice trailed off, as if he were embarrassed to say the rest of the sentence out loud.

"Say it, Seymour," the rabbi urged. "Finish your thought."

"That you weren't really running away," Pop murmured.

Well, I suppose that was true. I suppose I wasn't really running away. I found out a lot of things that night. I guess Pop found out a lot of things, too. It's wrong to keep all your feelings and ideas locked away. Pop and I both had a tendency to do that. We're alike that way.

There was one thing I didn't find out that night, though. I didn't find out why the rabbi had come to see me in the first place. That information had to wait for another day.

CHAPTER TWELVE |

The next morning, I slept and slept. I hadn't set my alarm, and my father didn't wake me up before he left for work. When I finally opened my eyes, the clock said ten-thirty. I threw on a pair of jeans and trotted downstairs. On the kitchen table I found a note.

> Dear Vic,
>   It's OK if you don't go to school today.
> You must be really beat. When I get home,
> I'll drive you over to pick up your bike.
> Luckily, it's a nice day.
>
> Pop.

A note from Pop. Well.

I ate some cereal and milk, and then I called the rabbi.

"So, listen, Rabbi," I said after Mrs. Kadin had connected us, "why did you come to see me last night?" I talked kind of casually to the rabbi; I wasn't so much in awe of him anymore. He and I and Pop had sat together in the middle of the night in my grandfather's workshop.

But when he answered, his voice was serious. "I'd heard about the shoplifting business," he said. "I knew then why you'd been so short with me on the phone Wednesday night. I came over to see if there was anything I could do to help."

So he wanted to help. Maybe he could. "Rabbi, if a Jew's done something wrong, he's still a Jew isn't he?" I asked, my voice as serious as his. "I mean, like that gangster who died down in Florida, Meyer Lansky."

"Yes, Lansky was a Jew until his last day," the rabbi sighed. "Not a good Jew, but a Jew. We Jews have no monopoly on saints, or sinners."

"Suppose a person who'd done something bad came to you and said he thought he was a Jew on the inside, and wanted to be one on the outside, too. Would you convert him?" Now we were getting to the crux of the matter.

And Rabbi Auerbach knew it. "Everyone's done bad things," he said. "Including the holiest men and women. Including even me," he added with a dry laugh. "If a requirement for being Jewish were perfection, there wouldn't be any Jews. Judaism, like all religions, exists to help flawed human beings through life."

"Would you convert a thief?" I'd said it. Thief. Up until now I'd just thought "shoplifter." But a shoplifter is a thief. There's no difference.

"Yes, I would," Rabbi Auerbach responded without a moment's hesitation. "I would convert a thief if that thief assured me he wasn't a thief anymore, and that he would never be a thief again." He stopped talking. I didn't say anything, either. "Do you hear me, Vic?" he asked.

"Yes, I hear you."

"Well, then, say it."

"Say what?"

"Repeat after me. I will never again . . ."

"I will never again . . ."

". . . so long as I live . . ."

". . . so long as I live . . ."

". . . take something that isn't mine."

". . . take something that isn't mine."

"So help me God."

"So help me God."

"It counts over the phone," the rabbi said. "It counts just as much as if you were standing on the bimah, by the open ark, in front of the Torah."

"I've given you my word, Rabbi." My father didn't believe me; my mother didn't believe me. Maybe he would.

"OK, Vic. I count this as the second time. You've asked me a second time."

"Yes, Rabbi. This was the second time."

"Goodbye, Vic."

"Goodbye, Rabbi."

After I hung up the phone, I thought a long time. I felt as if now I had committed myself. But I could still get out of it. I didn't have to ask the third time.

While Pop was driving me over to the workshop to

pick up my bike, I told him I was thinking about going through with the conversion.

"Don't expect a bar mitzvah," he retorted sharply. "You don't deserve a big party with a lot of presents."

"A bar mitzvah and a party are two different things," I said. "The bar mitzvah doesn't cost anything. No one has to give it to me, except the rabbi." I laughed a little. "It's funny, isn't it? A month ago, you were dead set on my bar mitzvah, and I was dead set against it. Times have changed." Then I added, "Maybe." I still wasn't sure. I wanted to be sure. I mean it was for my whole life.

I heard no more talk about going someplace else to live, but the mellow mood that had overtaken my father while he sat with the rabbi and me in my grandfather's old workshop sure didn't last. It faded markedly after our interview with the juvenile intake social worker and collapsed totally with the arrival of my summons to appear in Juvenile Court. As the hearing date approached, he grew angrier and angrier. By Tuesday, January 13, he wasn't speaking to me at all.

New Hebron is the county seat. The courthouse is only a short distance from where we live, thank God. I would have frozen to death if I'd had to drive in a car with him and his icy silence a moment longer than the ten minutes the trip took.

The judge wasn't ready for us when we arrived. We had to sit in an outer room waiting until we were called. Stewie was there, too, with his mother and father, but not Arnold. His parents had requested a hearing on another date.

Pop sat down as far away from Stewie and his folks

as he could get. I hesitated a moment and then I sat down next to Pop, whether he liked it or not. I didn't want to get involved in a conversation with Stewie or his father. In school a couple of days before, Stewie had said to me, "Listen. My old man and I talked it over. I'm going to plead not guilty. You better plead not guilty, too."

"Not guilty?" I exclaimed. I thought he'd lost the few marbles he still had left. "Not guilty? But we are guilty. I mean, they caught us red-handed. How can you plead not guilty?"

"It's my word against Lippman's."

"What about the cops?" I reminded him. "They were there, too."

Stewie dismissed them with a sneer. "They didn't see anything. Mr. Lippman already had the watch back by the time they came."

"But you confessed," I pointed out.

"That was under duress," Stewie replied airily.

Under duress? "Stewie," I said, "you're crazy."

"You mean you're not going to stick by me in this?" Stewie asked. He sounded positively amazed, as if he couldn't believe his own ears.

"Are you sticking by me?" I retorted. "I'll tell you my honest opinion. A contest between you and Lippman is no contest. Lippman's going to win. He's a respected businessman in town, and you're just a kid who gets into trouble."

Stewie shook his head. "That's not what my old man says. You'll be sorry you didn't stick with me. My old man says we'll get the . . . bastard."

Did he hesitate before he said "bastard"? Did he almost say "Jew bastard"? Maybe, with all that had happened lately, I was turning paranoid and just imagining things.

Pop and I had been sitting next to each other in perfect, unbroken silence for what seemed like half an hour, but couldn't actually have been more than ten minutes, when Stewie's father consulted briefly with Stewie and then got up and walked across the room toward us. "Well, Mr. Abrams," he said in a cheerful, hearty voice, "it looks like you and me have our hands full with these sons of ours." For a second, I thought he was actually going to slap Pop on the back. But Pop was in no mood to encourage familiarity. He only nodded briefly.

"Boys do get into mischief," Mr. Brisbane said, pulling out the chair next to Pop's and sitting down. "I think they're making a lot of fuss over nothing around here. Why aren't the cops out chasing real criminals instead of wasting time with a couple of harmless kids? That's what I want to know."

"Maybe they don't think stealing is harmless," Pop replied dryly. "Maybe they're worried about what it can lead to."

"A life of crime?" Mr. Brisbane laughed humorlessly. "Not for my boy. I'm not letting him get off to a bad start. I'm having him plead not guilty, and if I were you, I'd have your boy do the same."

"But he is guilty," Pop said. Those had been almost exactly my words to Stewie. "But we are guilty," I had said.

"It's their word against Lippman's," Mr. Brisbane said.

"If you were a judge, who would you believe?" Pop asked. "Especially if Lippman's telling the truth and the kids are lying?"

Mr. Brisbane turned to me. "Boy, you must have done something terrible to your father. He's sure out to get you."

Pop's face turned white and his hand clenched the arm of his chair. "I don't see it that way, Mr. Brisbane," I said. I laid my hand on the arm of my chair as I spoke. It was right next to Pop's.

"You guys stick together, don't you, Abrams?" Mr. Brisbane said, as if he hadn't even heard me. "You and Lippman. That's more important to you than your own son."

Pop's lips barely moved as he answered. "Are you going to go back to your family, or should I change my seat?"

Even Mr. Brisbane got the point. He stood up and walked away. Pop let out a long breath of air. "Thanks, Vic," he said. At least, I think that's what he said. His voice was so low I could barely make out his words.

Then the door leading from the courtroom into the antechamber where we were sitting opened. A sheriff's officer stood in the doorway. "The case of the State versus Stewart Brisbane is now called," he announced. I didn't think he had to speak quite so loud. It was a small room. We could all hear him. "The case of the State versus Victor Abrams is now called."

Stewie and his parents and Pop and I entered the

courtroom. The sheriff's officer led us to a table right up in front and told us to sit down. Then he marched to the judge's bench, turned around, and announced, "This court is now in session. Judge Eleanor O'Hara presiding. Please rise." Why had he made us sit if all he was going to do was make us get up again? He still spoke as if he had to make himself heard above the din of a huge crowd, when actually no one was in the whole place except the six of us.

We stood up. A door to the side opened and Judge O'Hara came through. She was a tall, white-haired, unsmiling woman dressed in a black robe. She carried a sheaf of papers. She sat down, glanced in our direction, and nodded briefly. Then we sat, too. She laid her papers out in front of her and examined them for several moments. The silence in the room was thick as cotton, thick as snow.

It was broken by the sound of a door opening. I turned to see who was coming into the courtroom. The principal of New Hebron Middle School? A reporter from the New Hebron *Gazette?* But it was no one like that—no one whose presence I half feared, half expected. It was Rabbi Auerbach. He walked purposefully toward us, smiling very faintly. He slid into the seat next to mine. "I'm sorry I'm late," he whispered. "I got held up." He sounded as if we'd been waiting for him. I didn't even know how he'd found out the date of the hearing. I turned toward my father and looked at him questioningly. Pop shrugged slightly and shook his head.

If Judge O'Hara noticed Rabbi Auerbach's arrival,

she evinced neither surprise nor interest. "Stewart Brisbane," she said, "please approach the bench." Stewie swaggered forward, chin up, shoulders back, just the opposite from the way he had walked out of Lippman's with the cops.

The sheriff's officer approached him, carrying a black volume. "Put your left hand on the Bible," he said. "Raise your right hand. Do you swear to tell the truth, the whole truth, and nothing but the truth?"

Stewie nodded.

"Say 'I do,'" the officer insisted.

"I do," Stewie repeated.

The officer sat down. Stewie moved toward the witness's chair, as if he, too, were about to sit down.

"Remain standing," Judge O'Hara ordered.

Stewie remained standing, his shoulders just a little hunched now.

"You stand accused of petty larceny," Judge O'Hara said. "How do you plead, guilty or not guilty?"

"Not guilty," Stewie said. I could hardly hear him.

"What did you say?" the judge asked sharply.

"Not guilty," Stewie said, a little louder this time.

Judge O'Hara looked puzzled. She glanced in the direction of Mr. and Mrs. Brisbane. "That's right," Mr. Brisbane's voice boomed out. "Not guilty."

Judge O'Hara's eyebrows shot up. "You understand that means the boy will now have to stand trial," she said.

"Yes," Mr. Brisbane said.

"He will require counsel," Judge O'Hara said.

"What?" Mr. Brisbane asked.

"He'll need a lawyer. You'll have to hire a lawyer."

Now Mr. Brisbane looked puzzled. "Can't the court provide a lawyer?" he asked.

"Are you claiming indigence?" Judge O'Hara queried.

"Stewart has no money," Mr. Brisbane said.

"According to the statutes of this state, it is the obligation of the parents to provide the lawyer," Judge O'-Hara responded firmly, "unless they're too poor to pay the fee."

"Well . . ." Mr. Brisbane seemed to hesitate.

But Judge O'Hara had no time to waste. "If you decide to claim indigence, see the clerk on your way out. She'll give you the proper forms," she said. She turned to Stewie. "You're sure of your plea?" she asked. "You can still change it."

"Not guilty," he repeated.

"All right," she said. She sounded very tired. "You'll receive notice of your trial date in the mail. In the meantime, I release you in the custody of your parents. Mr. Brisbane, Mrs. Brisbane, you will be held personally responsible if Stewart does not appear."

"I guarantee it," Mr. Brisbane said, his voice rising. "I guarantee his appearance. He's not going anywhere. You better believe he's not going anywhere."

"And you?" the judge asked coolly.

"How can I go anywhere?" He sounded almost bitter. "I have a job; I have a family."

Judge O'Hara's face was grim, but she merely said, "You will be notified of the trial date. You're dismissed."

"That's all?" Stewie asked.

Judge O'Hara's frown deepened. "That's all," she said, ". . . for now."

Stewie and his mother and father left the courtroom. His father's jovial manner had entirely disappeared. He grabbed Stewie by the upper arm and practically shoved him out of the room. "Cripes, Pa," Stewie complained as he stumbled through the door, "you don't have to push me. I'm not going to run away." I didn't hear what his father said in reply, if anything, for the door shut behind them.

"Victor Abrams," Judge O'Hara said. "Please approach the bench."

Knees shaking, palms sweating, I managed to move forward. I kept my shoulders back and my chin up, too. I made sure I looked a lot better than I felt.

The sheriff's officer made me swear to tell the truth. Then the judge asked me if I pled guilty or not guilty to the charge of petty larceny.

"I'm no thief," I replied. "I shoplifted."

Judge O'Hara's mouth softened a little. "Do you really think there's a difference?" she asked, raising her eyebrows.

I shook my head slowly.

"Then how do you plead?" she repeated. "Guilty or not guilty?"

"Guilty," I replied quietly.

She heard me. "Very well," she said. "In view of the reports of the police and the juvenile intake officer, which I just finished reading, that certainly seems the wisest plea. Nothing remains, then, but to impose a sentence."

I stood there, waiting.

"May I have the court's permission to say something?" Rabbi Auerbach rose and spoke in a clear, strong voice.

"Ah, yes, Rabbi Auerbach," Judge O'Hara said. "I know you requested permission to be present today. May I ask why?"

"I'm Vic's clergyman," he replied. "I'd like to say a few words on his behalf, prior to your sentencing him. They may make a difference."

"Certainly, Rabbi," Judge O'Hara said. "The court will be pleased to hear you."

The sheriff's officer didn't swear the rabbi in. Judge O'Hara simply let him talk.

"I just want to tell you," Rabbi Auerbach said, "what I think of the defendant."

That was me. The defendant.

"He didn't ask me to come here today," Rabbi Auerbach went on. "Neither did his father. It was entirely my own idea. This is the boy's first offense."

"I know," Judge O'Hara interrupted. "Rabbi Auerbach, I assure you it's not our policy to incarcerate first offenders, especially when they're juveniles. However, I must point out to you that according to our intake officer's report, young Mr. Abrams has a long history of truancy, fighting, and other acts evidencing a lack of respect for authority."

"Your honor, that's why I'm here," Rabbi Auerbach explained. "I want to tell you that it's obvious to me that in the last few weeks this boy's behavior has undergone a remarkable change."

What was Rabbi Auerbach talking about? I had

changed? How? That's what I felt like asking him. But I didn't. I kept my mouth shut.

The rabbi went on. "He has voluntarily started to attend synagogue services on Saturday mornings. The only fighting he's been involved in lately has been worthy defense of those under attack. He has expressed to me a desire to pursue a Jewish education. Above all, he has absolutely sworn to me that he will never, never again, as long as he lives, take something that does not belong to him. Judge O'Hara, I believe him. Whatever it says on those papers in front of you, it doesn't say that he has the reputation of a liar."

"It doesn't say that," Judge O'Hara agreed. "And it says also that somehow he always managed to get good grades. Thank you, Rabbi."

I think Rabbi Auerbach would have liked to say more, but he couldn't very well ignore Judge O'Hara's obvious dismissal. She was as good at ending conversations as he was. He sat down, and she turned to me. "Victor Abrams," she began.

"Yes, Your Honor," I replied.

"You understand you've been charged with a serious crime."

"Yes, ma'am."

"An adult so accused could receive a maximum sentence of five years in jail. The fact that you are a juvenile affects your punishment, but it in no way mitigates the offense. Stealing is stealing."

"Yes, ma'am."

"Did you mean what you told the rabbi? You will never, ever do anything like this again?"

"Yes, ma'am." I put all the strength of which I was capable into my reply.

"Then I sentence you to one year's probation," she announced. "When you leave here, you will report to the Juvenile Bureau, where you had your interview with the intake social worker. There you will find out who your probation officer is and how often you must report." Next she addressed the sheriff's officer. "I wish to be kept informed of this boy's progress," she said. "If he misses a meeting with his probation officer, or if he gets into any kind of trouble whatsoever, in school, or at home, or anywhere else, I want to know about it. Is that clear?"

"Yes, Your Honor," the sheriff's officer responded.

"Very well. Dismissed."

I stared at her. She stared back at me. "Dismissed," she repeated. This time she smiled.

Pop, Rabbi Auerbach, and I walked out of the courtroom together. "Thanks for coming, Rabbi," Pop said.

"Well," he replied, "I wanted to come. I don't think my being here made any difference. She'd have sentenced you to a year's probation anyway."

"It made a difference to me," I said.

Outside the courthouse, Pop headed toward the County Building across the street. I lingered behind for a moment. "Will you convert me, Rabbi?" I asked. This was the third time.

"It's tough to be a Jew," the rabbi replied.

"I already am a Jew," I said. "Inside, where it counts."

"We'll talk about it," he said. "Come to see me tomorrow after school."

Pop was standing by the curb. "Hey, Vic," he called, "come on, hurry up. The day doesn't have to be a total loss. I still have time to get some work done at the office."

I loped toward him along the sidewalk. A year's probation. That wasn't so bad. It could have been worse. It could have been a lot worse.

How much worse, I found out later. Stewie was tried, found guilty, and sentenced to three years' probation. Three years. And Arnold was sent away to Long Hill Farm because it was his fourth offense. So I was lucky, and I knew it.

CHAPTER THIRTEEN |

One morning about a month later, I again got up early to catch Pop before he went to work. I came downstairs to find him drinking his coffee and reading the newspaper, the same as always. "Listen, Pop," I said, "I want you to know. Today's the day."

He lowered his newspaper and stared at me. "The day? What day?"

"I'm getting converted today," I said. "Remember? The little cut, and the dip in the mikvah?"

"Oh, yeah." He laid the newspaper on the table. "I still haven't changed my mind about the bar mitzvah," he said. "No bar mitzvah parties for you."

What was the use? I turned away from him and walked over to the refrigerator. I knew there was a carton of orange juice in there. I'd bought it myself the day before.

He was still talking. "You've been behaving lately, though. I talked to your probation officer. She's satisfied."

All right. A little better. I brought the carton of juice and a glass to the table and sat down. "Now that I'm back in Hebrew School, I don't have much time for trouble," I explained. "I mean, it takes all my energy just to be civil to Mr. Hyman, like I promised Rabbi Auerbach."

Pop reached into his pocket, pulled out his wallet, and peeled off twenty dollars. "I'm giving you back your allowance."

"Thanks, Pop," I said as he handed me the money. It was amazing to me how well I'd managed without it. What I'd actually done was taken over the grocery shopping, seen to it there was some decent food in the house, packed a lunch each morning, and saved the lunch money that he kept giving me all along to use when I needed cash. Pop must have known what I was doing. He could see the packages of bologna, the loaves of rye bread, and the Hostess Twinkies sitting in the refrigerator just as well as I could. So I had figured what I was doing was OK with him.

And, of course, there'd been no time to spend much money. Besides Hebrew School, I had private lessons twice a week with Cantor Itkin, to catch up. They were much better than Hebrew School. The cantor was a nice guy in his middle twenties. He had all kinds of jazzy tunes for different parts of the service, and he taught them to me. He taught them to all the bar mitzvah kids. Thanks to him, I could now also find my place in the prayer book.

I went to a bar or bat mitzvah almost every weekend. Some weekends there were two, one Friday night and one Saturday morning. I was always invited, whether the parents liked the idea or not. I went to Howie's and Morty's and Debbie Barton's. I called my mother to find out what to get for Debbie. Mom asked me if her ears were pierced. When she asked me that, I remembered. "I know, I know," I exclaimed. "I know what Debbie wants. Ivory earrings that look like little flowers." Mom went out and got them. She paid for them, too. She knew I wasn't getting any allowance. Debbie liked them a lot.

At the parties, all the kids treated me the same as they always had, except Abby. She still wasn't talking to me. During the services, the cantor always invited the whole bar mitzvah class to come up to the bimah to chant some of the prayers to the tunes he'd taught us. We were like a choir. Abby always stood as far away from me as she could. After the first couple of times, I realized she was doing that on purpose.

I usually didn't have time in the morning for anything more than a glass of juice, but the day of my conversion I was awake so early that I had time to eat. I got up from the table to make myself some raisin toast when Pop spoke to me. "What time is that ceremony?" he asked.

"Four o'clock," I said. "The rabbi's driving me over." I looked at him steadily. "You could meet us there. It's halfway between here and the city. You could take the car in today, and then meet us there." I kept my voice cool. I didn't want to sound as if I was begging. But he had put down his newspaper. He had asked me what time. I figured it was OK, then, to invite him.

He nodded slowly. "All right," he said seriously, "I'll be there." Then he smiled. "After that we'll have supper together at the kosher deli. That's the right place to celebrate becoming Jewish, don't you think?"

"Yeah, Pop," I said. "That's a good idea."

"You can ask the rabbi if he wants to come along, too," Pop said. "My treat."

"And Morty and Howie?" I asked.

"Morty and Howie?" he repeated.

"They're my witnesses," I explained. "You have to have three, but the rabbi makes the third. Usually he picks the other two, to make sure they're qualified Jewish men. But he let me pick my own. I didn't know if they would want to come, but they were very pleased to be invited. They feel kind of like godfathers."

Pop sort of grunted. It suddenly occurred to me that he was disappointed, maybe jealous even, because I hadn't asked him. "You can't have your father," I explained hastily. "At a brit, when you're born, your father is not your godfather. That wouldn't make any sense." I didn't know if that was true, but it certainly sounded reasonable.

Pop nodded. I could see he felt better. "Of course, Morty and Howie, too," he said. "It'll be a regular party."

It was. The mikvah was part of an Orthodox day

school in Bayport. It had no parking lot because it was the kind of school to which most everyone walked. In the middle of the day, it wasn't easy to find a parking place in the neighborhood, which was full of shabby appliance stores and auto-body repair shops. We had to park three blocks away and, by the time we walked over to the mikvah, we found Pop standing in the doorway waiting for us and looking vaguely uncomfortable. I braced myself for the lecture about making him leave his office early and wasting his time, but it didn't come —maybe because Rabbi Auerbach was with me. The cantor had wanted to come along, too, but he had pupils that afternoon.

Inside we were greeted by the shammes, the caretaker. He led us to a little room fitted out with a few worn chairs, covered in make-believe leather, and an examining table, like the kind you see in doctors' offices. "Hokay, young fella," the shammes said. "Get yourself up on that table and lie down." I didn't like him at all. It seemed to me that his smile as he spoke was sly and secret. I could almost imagine him rubbing his hands together in delight at the prospect of the pain I was soon to experience. I was sure it was going to hurt a lot. Rabbi Auerbach had told me a thousand times that it wouldn't, but I didn't believe him. I was nervous, all right, and that shammes didn't help.

Neither did Morty and Howie. They were kind of nervous, too, and giggled at every sentence out of that shammes's mouth, as if he were *Mad* magazine come to life. "Maybe you'll survive," Howie said as I lay down. That was his idea of a joke.

"Maybe even intact," Morty added. He was less funny than Howie, if such a thing was possible. I could feel beads of sweat forming on my forehead.

"That's enough," Pop said sharply. "This is a serious occasion." Mercifully, Howie and Morty shut up.

I closed my eyes. I could hear the rabbi moving around, opening his case, rattling objects. Then his footsteps came toward me. Everyone else was perfectly still, perfectly silent.

The rabbi began to chant softly in Hebrew. Afterward he repeated what he had said in English. I think that was for Pop's benefit, because he had certainly explained to me and to Morty and Howie many times in advance all that he was going to do and say. "We praise You, O Lord our God," he translated, "King of the universe, who has commanded us concerning the circumcision of non-Jews. You are blessed, O Lord our God, who establishes this covenant." Then I felt a sharp nick. It did hurt. It hurt a lot. But it was over very, very fast. I braced myself for what was coming next. But nothing else came. I opened my eyes. My father was standing next to me, a book in his hand. "You are blessed, O Lord our God, King of the universe," Pop read, "who has made us holy by Your commandments, and has commanded us to make our sons enter into the covenant of Abraham our father."

The rabbi hadn't mentioned anything about that part —but he hadn't known my father would be there. He must have stuck it in at the last minute.

"It hurt," I said, "but it didn't hurt long."

"That's good," the rabbi said.

I didn't know if it was so good. I felt a little disappointed. Maybe I'd expected to go through some terrible ordeal. Maybe part of me wanted a terrible ordeal.

But I remembered something the rabbi had told me in one of our study sessions. "There are all kinds of pain. Once physical pain is over, we tend to forget about it. Mental pain isn't erased so easily."

Well, then, perhaps I'd experienced my ordeal before I'd even walked into that room. Maybe it had been enough.

The shammes led us down into the basement. We entered a small room filled with a little tile pool. The walls of the room were tiled, too, and so was the edging, about a foot wide, around the mikvah. I took off all of my clothes and walked down the steps into the water, which came up to about the middle of my chest. Then I said my part, in Hebrew and English. I'd memorized it. "We praise You, O Lord our God, King of the universe, who has made us holy by Your commandments and commanded us concerning immersion."

The rabbi, my father, the shammes, Morty, and Howie all said, "Amen."

"Now dunk," said the shammes. "Dunk all the way. Don't let a single hair on your head stick out of the water." The shammes wanted to make sure everything was kosher. I know he didn't trust Morty or Howie, and he probably didn't trust the rabbi, either.

I remembered not to hold my nose or close my eyes as I sank down into the water. Blowing bubbles, I counted to ten while I was beneath the surface, just to make sure. When I came up, I shook my head to get the water out of my nose and ears and eyes. Then I said, "Blessed are You, O Lord our God, King of the universe, who has kept us in life, and has preserved us, and has enabled us to reach this special day."

Again everyone else in the room said, "Amen."

"That was very good, sonny," the shammes said. "Now, twice more. Dunk twice more, just like you did before."

So I dunked twice more. Then I came out of the water. The shammes handed me a towel so I could dry myself off. He smiled at me, so I smiled back. His smile seemed nice enough this time.

While I was rubbing myself with the towel, the rabbi said, "In token of your admission into this covenant of Israel, we welcome you by giving you the name of Avigdor ben Shlomo, by which you shall be known among the people of Israel." That was my official Hebrew name, Avigdor ben Shlomo, which could be translated as Victor, son of Seymour.

I put on my clothes and we all went back upstairs. In the room where the hatafat dam brit had taken place, the rabbi gave me a certificate. "Read it carefully before you sign it," he said.

I read it. This is what it said:

> I hereby declare my desire to accept the
> principles of the Jewish religion, to
> follow its practices and ceremonies, and
> to become a member of the Jewish people.
> I do this of my own free will, with an
> understanding of the significance of the

tenets and practices of Judaism and full
realization of the commitment I herewith
assume.

I pray that my present conviction may
guide me through life, that I may be
worthy of the sacred tradition and fellowship
which I now join. As I am
thankful for the privileges thus bestowed
upon me, I pray that I may always
remain conscious of the duties which
are mine as a member of the House of
Israel.

I declare my determination to maintain
a Jewish home. Should I be blessed
with male children, I pledge to bring
them into the Covenant of Abraham.
I further pledge to rear all children
with whom God may bless me in loyalty
to the Jewish faith and its practices.

Hear, O Israel: the Lord is our God,
the Lord Alone. Praised be His
Sovereign glory forever.

"That's fine," I announced when I had finished reading it. The rabbi handed me a pen, and I signed it. Then
he signed it, and Morty signed it, and Howie signed it.
It was all legal now. It was all official.

"That's all?" Howie asked. "That's the whole megil-
lah?"

"That's all," the rabbi agreed. "It's what comes before that's hard. Before and after." He shook my hand. "Congratulations, Avigdor ben Shlomo. I'm very happy."

"So am I." That was Pop. He shook my hand, too. So did Morty. So did Howie. So did the shammes. The shammes also shook Pop's hand, and Pop slipped him a five-dollar bill. Then we left.

The rabbi said he couldn't have supper with us. His wife was waiting for him at home. He drove off in his own car, and Pop, Morty, Howie, and I went to the kosher deli. It was known as the best kosher deli in the whole state. We consumed bowls of chicken soup with matzah balls and big, fat combination pastrami and corned-beef sandwiches on rye bread with mustard and side orders of cole slaw and french fried potatoes. Howie and Morty ordered Cokes, but I had cream soda and Pop drank celery tonic. "I'll have heartburn for a week," he said, "but it's worth it."

"You should have watched, Vic," Morty said. "You shouldn't have closed your eyes. You shouldn't have missed the sight of the rabbi standing over you with that knife."

"Was it a big knife?" I asked.

"Oh, huge," Morty said. He spread his hands at least a foot apart.

Pop laughed, and I knew that Morty was lying. I had known it anyway.

"I'm lucky he has a steady hand," I said.

"Oh, it didn't look so steady to me," Howie said. "He was shaking like anything. He's not used to doing circumcisions, you know. He isn't the regular mohel. For babies they bring in a guy from the city."

"The one who did Howie must have been drunk," Morty said.

Howie responded in kind. From there on, the conversation degenerated. Howie and Morty's remarks got grosser and grosser. Pop told every joke he'd ever heard about circumcision, mohels, and the male anatomy. What hadn't struck me as the least bit funny when I was lying on the table now appeared to be wildly hysterical. By the time we got to the strudel and tea, the four of us were laughing so hard we nearly wet our pants.

We drove home. Pop dropped Howie off first, and then Morty. When we got back to our house, Pop said to me, "Boy, Vic, your friends talk pretty rough. It was a good thing the rabbi didn't come out with us after all."

"If he'd been there," I pointed out, "the conversation would never have taken place."

Pop laughed. "I guess not," he agreed.

"You did all right yourself, Pop," I reminded him. "I mean, I never heard half those jokes before. Where did you get the one about the shmekelectomy?"

Pop shrugged. "Think I remember? I seem to have known it all my life. Maybe my father told it to me."

Grandpa. Maybe he had. "I'm glad you were there, Pop," I said. "It wouldn't have been right without you."

"Well, I wouldn't have missed it for anything," he replied. Now his eyes were serious, his voice hesitant and quiet. "I want to come to your bar mitzvah, too. And you should invite your mother. I think she'll want to be there. We'll just have a Kiddush afterwards, right in the temple, and then Saturday night you can take all your friends roller skating or bowling or something like that."

"Maybe I'll take them swimming in the mikvah," I suggested.

He smiled again and touched my arm. "Vic," he said, "there're too many of them. They'll never fit."

No big party. No pompous uncles, no bejeweled aunts, no smug, self-satisfied cousins. Thank God. The thought of my conversion had made me nervous. My bar mitzvah I was actually looking forward to.

CHAPTER FOURTEEN |

"No," Pop said. "I'm not going to order fancy printed invitations. It's not that kind of affair. Mother, I want you to understand something. It's not going to be like Craig's bar mitzvah, or Allen's."

"Then it should be on a Monday or Thursday morning," Grandma said, plopping a pale, bluish piece of chicken on Pop's plate. "So no one will notice."

They took the Torah out on Monday and Thursday as well as Saturday mornings, but I didn't want a weekday bar mitzvah. "I want my friends to come," I protested. "They can't come on a Thursday. I don't want it during the week, as if someone had just died."

"Well, then," Grandma said, "you should send out invitations and have some of my friends, too. What were you planning to do?" she asked Pop sharply. "Just call your brothers up on the phone and tell them to come?"

"They don't have to come if they don't want to," I said quickly. "They really don't even have to know about it."

She shot me a withering glance. "Your uncles?" she said. "Your cousins? They don't have to know about it? You want me to keep it a secret, but you won't have it during the week. Make up your mind. One way or the other."

"Did I say it was a secret, Mother?" Pop was clearly annoyed. "It's no secret."

"What're you, ashamed of him or something?" she asked. She knew about the shoplifting and the probation officer I visited every month and all the rest of it. She hadn't been too upset when she'd found out. She'd acted as if it was no more than she'd expected all along.

Pop didn't answer her.

"You shouldn't be," Grandma went on. I was carrying a forkful of burnt kugle to my mouth. I put my loaded fork back down on my plate and turned my face in her direction. This I really had to hear. "He's actually been a very good boy lately."

"Grandma," I asked, overcome by curiosity, "what makes you say that?"

"Oh," she replied casually, "everyone knows. They all talk about it. The rabbi, the cantor, Mrs. Greenglass."

"Mrs. Greenglass?" That was a surprise. Abby still didn't speak to me.

"Mrs. Greenglass belongs to the stock club, too,"

Grandma explained. "Everyone in the stock club knows you're a reformed character. Even Mrs. Lippman."

The last thing I needed around New Hebron Middle School was a reputation for saintliness. Maybe I had carried good behavior in Mr. Hyman's Hebrew School class too far. I really didn't want my label to be "apple polisher" any more than I wanted it to be "shoplifter." "Cool kid" was what I wanted, if I had to have a label at all. Actually, the best thing would be to be rid of labels entirely. They only get in the way of your freedom. Anyway, I sincerely hoped the news of my reformation hadn't spread too far beyond the synagogue and the stock club.

"Will you have some string beans?" Grandma asked me.

"No, thanks," I said. Grandma's string beans were canned.

She directed the serving spoon of string beans toward her own plate, changed her mind, and dropped it back in the bowl, which was as full of string beans in the middle of the meal as it had been at the beginning. "I'm a lousy cook," she said, "but I'm handy." That was true. Her house, and our house too, was full of needlepoint pillows and crocheted afghans that she had made over the years. To me they were silly, like doilies on sofa arms, but I guess a person who likes that kind of thing would consider them well made. She fastened her eyes on my face. "Vic, did you know I did calligraphy?"

I shook my head. "No, Grandma."

"When the boys had their bar mitzvahs and were

married, I addressed all the envelopes. I'll address yours, too," she added, "and I'll also write the invitation up—something informal. A bar mitzvah and a little Kiddush. That's all. And I'll take it down to the fast print place and they'll make copies."

I glanced at my father. He nodded. "OK, Grandma," I said. "That would be nice."

"Seymour, just tell me how many," she said. "I'll give you my list tomorrow."

Pop knew when he was licked. "A hundred will be plenty," he said.

It was more than enough. After the invitations were mailed off, I took one of the extras, put it in an envelope, and took it with me to school. It was for Abby. I was going to make it very hard for her to turn me down. I wanted her to squirm a little.

I waited for her outside the door to the home ec room. When she walked out, she saw me. She was going to walk right by me, as usual, but I said, very loud, so everyone could hear me, "Abby!"

She had to stop. But she didn't say anything. A couple of other kids stopped, too, and stared at us. I waited until they'd moved away. Then I said, "You go to social studies now. I'll walk you."

Still saying nothing, she moved away. I fell in step beside her. I opened my math book, pulled out the envelope with her name on it, and held it out to her. "This is for you," I said. "It's an invitation to my bar mitzvah."

She spoke at last. "Keep it," she said. "We got one at the house. It was addressed to the whole family."

"This one is for you personally," I replied.

"I'm not coming," she said. "I'm busy that day."

"You are not busy," I said. I kept my voice low and calm, but it was an effort. "You're so big on honesty. At least tell me the real reason."

"You know the real reason," she said. "You're a phony, Victor Abrams. All this Jewish business all of a sudden—it's an act. For your probation officer's benefit, I guess. So you'll be done with her sooner, and can go back to being what you really are."

I stopped walking. I put my hand on her arm so she had to stop, too. "You know what's going on inside of me, Abby?" I asked. "You know what I'm really feeling? You can tell when I'm acting out my true feelings and when I'm not? What makes you think you're qualified to be judge of the world?" I let the invitation drop out of my hand and onto the floor. "Who died, Abby, and named you God in his will?"

She stared at me. "Leave me alone, Vic Abrams," she whispered. "I hate you. I hate you. I'm sorry now I kept those stuffed mice. When I get home, I'm going to throw them away."

I was stunned. I was so surprised that all the anger washed out of me. "You kept those stuffed mice?" I asked. "Those mice I gave you to be a prize for the Young Judaea Israeli cafe? You *kept* them?"

Her mouth fell open, but no sounds came out of it.

"You know what that was, don't you?" I asked her. "Don't you?"

"Yes," she replied softly. "Stealing. It was stealing. I stole from Young Judaea." One thing about Abby—she didn't run away from the truth, not even when it hurt her.

"I'm not going to blame you for that, Abby." My voice was as thick as maple syrup. "I'm not going to hold it against you. I'm not even going to remember it."

"Thanks, Vic," Abby said. She said it so quietly I could hardly hear her. Then she turned from me and walked away slowly. Her shoulders were hunched and shaking. I thought maybe she was crying. No matter what had happened before, she had never cried. I felt a little bad. But not too bad. Like I said, I don't need to be a martyr or a saint.

For the next couple of weeks I was very busy. I had to see the cantor nearly every day. My actual birthday was March 29, but we were all too occupied to take much notice of it. Everyone who'd been invited to the bar mitzvah was coming, except the uncles, aunts, and cousins from out of town. I guess they'd decided it wasn't worth the trip just for Kiddush. That didn't upset me. Pop and Grandma were really mad, though.

Nine o'clock, Saturday morning, April 18, and there I was, seated on the bimah, wearing a suit and tie. I even had on a shirt with French cuffs. I finally had a chance to wear one of the pairs of cuff links sitting in the box on my bureau. I could only wear one set at a time, however—and now I had four new sets, which I'd received as bar mitzvah gifts. People are crazy, giving a kid cuff links. But I'd gotten some good presents, too, like a digital watch that was also a little calculator and lots of records and tapes. Most people had given me savings bonds or checks, and that was OK, too.

The cantor led shakrit, the early morning service. Slowly the sanctuary filled up. I was amazed at some of the people who appeared, people we hadn't even invited, like my probation officer. I didn't mind, though. Anyone can come into a synagogue, and I knew there was plenty of food. Pop had hired Mrs. Harter and a friend of hers who did some catering to fix the Kiddush.

It was time for the Torah service. The rabbi beckoned to me. I stood with him in front of the ark. He lifted out a scroll and handed it to me. I carried it around the synagogue, the rabbi, the cantor, and Mr. Gottman, the president of Congregation Brit Israel, walking behind me. I made sure everyone who wanted to had a chance to touch the Torah, no matter where they were sitting.

When Pop was called up to recite the blessing before the Torah reading, he did very well. I had made him practice a couple of times at home, and it was a good thing, too. It had been years since he'd stood in front of the Torah.

I read from the Torah. I chanted the haftarah. I led the whole Musaf service—the additional service that follows the reading of the Torah on a Saturday morning. I could do all that because Cantor Itkin had taught me. Besides, by that time, I'd been to about fifteen bar and bat mitzvahs in my class. I'd gotten so used to going to shul on Saturday mornings that I went sometimes even when there wasn't a bar mitzvah. It had gotten to be like a habit. You'd have to be pretty dumb to sit there Shabbat after Shabbat and not be able to figure out what was going on.

At the end of Musaf the rabbi made a little speech. He didn't say too much—just that he was proud of me and the distance that I had traveled in the past six months. He didn't go into detail. He didn't mention shoplifting; he didn't mention conversion. But I knew what he was talking about, and so did a lot of other people in that room.

Then he called my father and my mother to the bimah. They stood on either side of me. My father said a prayer in Hebrew. We'd practiced that one, too. My mother read it in English. It was the same one I'd said standing in the mikvah the day of my conversion. "Blessed are You, O Lord our God, King of the universe, who has kept us in life, and has preserved us, and has enabled us to reach this special day." She kissed me, and so did Pop, right there in front of everyone.

The three of us walked off the bimah together. She sat down next to Bart in the front row on the right side of the synagogue. Pop moved toward my grandmother and Mrs. Kirsch on the left side of the synagogue. I was confused. I didn't know where to go.

"Vic," the rabbi called. "Come back up here. You're not off the hook yet." Laughter rippled through the synagogue. The previous moments had been so serious, everyone was glad of the opportunity to smile.

I went back up on the bimah. "Go ahead, Vic," the cantor said. "You did the hard part. Now do the easy part."

"Call the others up," I said. "You know, like you always do."

The cantor nodded. He spoke into the microphone. "Vic would like his friends from his class to join him on the bimah." The class had been waiting for that moment. They had been sitting together, and they were ready. They gathered around the cantor and me at the cantor's reading desk.

I looked out in front of me. Pat and Big John were grinning at me from the third row. Stewie was there, too. At the last minute I had decided to invite him, even if he was a jerk. I mean, I *had* known him since fourth grade.

I looked to my right. Morty was standing next to me, and next to him was Howie. A girl was standing on my left; I could sense it. I glanced out of the corner of my eye to see who it was, and then I turned and looked her full in the face. I hadn't seen her before, when I'd carried the Torah around the room. It was Abby.

"Good job," she whispered. "You were terrific. You were the best."

"Thanks," I murmured.

My hand was resting on the open prayer book. Fleetingly she brushed it with her index finger. Her touch was so quick, so light, I wasn't really sure it had happened.

We sang the closing hymn. "Adon olam," we chanted together. "Lord of the world."

I knew the words we were singing. I knew what they meant. And for that moment, at least, I felt that they were true.

B'yado afkeed roohee
B'eit ee-shan v'ah-ee'rah

V'im roohee g'veeyahtee
Adonai lee v'lo eerah.

I give my soul into God's hand.
When I am asleep and when I am awake
God is with me, body and soul.
I will not be afraid.

ABOUT THE AUTHOR |

BARBARA COHEN, perhaps best known for that little classic *The Carp in the Bathtub*, is also highly regarded for her novels, which include *Thank You*, *Jackie Robinson*, *Bitter Herbs and Honey*, *The Innkeeper's Daughter*, and *Queen for a Day*. She is also the author of *I Am Joseph*, an ALA Notable Book, and *The Binding of Isaac*, both illustrated by Charles Mikolaycak; as well as *Yussel's Prayer*, also an ALA Notable Book, with pictures by Michael J. Deraney. In recognition of her outstanding contribution to Jewish literature for children and young people, the Association of Jewish Libraries recently presented Mrs. Cohen with their Sydney Taylor Body-of-Work Award.

Temple Israel
Minneapolis, Minnesota

IN HONOR OF THE BAR MITZVAH OF
TODD MARKER
FROM
MARILYN & JERRY MARKER